Because You Said So

Arlie Undercover Book Five

by

Dani Haviland

USA Today Bestselling Author

Book Description

Because you said so. Sometimes that's all it takes: trust and faith.

Undercover Detective Arlie has his hands full again. Two very pregnant women, an overeager protégé, and a new arrival bent on making Anchorage the human trafficking hub of the world. Will he be able to handle all of them and still wear the Santa suit?

Dedication

This book is dedicated to those who fight for the weak, especially when it's with great personal sacrifice. I urge everyone to be an advocate. Stay informed and be generous with your compassion. You never know when someone you love will need it.

Praise and Awards

Praise and Awards

USA Today Bestselling Author

Kindle Top 100 Bestselling Author

Amazon Top 100 Historical fiction authors

"There wasn't a heartstring this one didn't pull at! And, no spoilers, but that's one of the nicest endings I could have imagined – all round, proving redemption's possible, some things will last forever, and …. Karma. This isn't just a story of Jose and Loren; it's so much more. Amazon reader on *Too Fast for You* (http://bit.ly/2fast4YOU)

"From the picturesque descriptions of the Alaskan wilderness, to weaving a beautiful love story, the author's writing style is both serious and quirky. A perfect, relaxing read!" Amazon review of *One Arctic Summer* (http://bit.ly/2OneArcticSummer)

Chapter 1: Waiting and Waiting

Stats on Twins:
The chance of having twins is about 1 in 250 pregnancies. Identical twins are relatively rare, about 3 or 4 per 1000 live births. Identical twins have the exact same DNA and are therefore both the same gender and look alike. Fraternal twins are more common, especially when fertility drugs are used. These twins are no more alike (except for age) than two other siblings. They are created by two eggs and two sperm. Women of an 'advanced maternal age' (over 35), who are taller than average (5' 3 ¾"), are African American, and have a BMI over 30 are also more likely to deliver twins.

Early December

"Settle down, boys," Charlene said. "Here. I brought some books for you to read."

Chip and Carlos grinned, then disengaged from their latest thumb-wrestling match. "To be continued," Chip said.

"Yeah," his six-year-old brother agreed.

"They're very well-behaved," said the young pregnant woman next to her.

"Oomph!" Charlene exclaimed, grasping her side. "This girl has a kick! Oh, yes, those two keep each other entertained, for sure. Once they get started in any competition, though, they don't want to stop until one has proved dominance, victory or cried uncle or whatever the game or event requires. Hi, I'm Charlene. Due Christmas Day, give or take a few."

"Rita, same time. So, sounds like we're both having girls? Zodiac twins, as they say."

"I guess so. Is this your first?"

Rita rolled her eyes. "First, last, only. I'll never make that mistake again!" she said and huffed, a sudden frown clouding her previously perky demeanor.

"Children aren't mistakes. Surprises, maybe," Charlene offered gently.

"Yeah, well, I've seen you in here before," Rita said. "With your husband. At least that's one mistake I never made."

Charlene's eyes widened in shock. She was too stunned to speak, but her one-word gasp of indignation was impossible to contain. "What?"

"Oh," Rita said, blushing. "I'm so sorry. That sounded rude. Your husband — he is your husband, right? — seems like a charming man. I thought this was his first pregnancy by his glow, but it's obvious the twins are his. The boys look just like him." Rita squirmed in her seat, trying for a more comfortable position. "Marriage is fine, and I hope to be married one day. But to the right woman," she added, shrugging one shoulder and adding a wink.

"Huh? Oh… So you had a weak moment?" Charlene asked as Rita's blush moved to her face.

"Yeah. And for him, too. We met at the liquor store. He had just had his first major argument or spat or whatever with his boyfriend, and my girlfriend just dumped me. She split without a see ya, been nice, or go to hell. Since neither of us wanted to go home or drink alone, we split the bill for a hotel room and got plastered. Talk about a dumb mistake…"

"You're going to have to stop beating yourself up over that. Your daughter was meant to be, one way or another. Whether," Charlene tipped her head skywards, "someone up there decided you needed a baby or someone else needed this baby, she's coming into this world for a reason. So, did you and your girlfriend make up? Or the baby daddy and his boyfriend?"

"Nope and I don't know. Kitty's out of my life for good now. She's gone underground, invisible or to China. Whatever or wherever. She's too ornery for anyone. The relationship with her was exciting at the time. I was brought up in a conservative home and had just recently come 'out.' As far as the guy, who knows? Baby daddy was a one-night stand. I don't even know his real name."

"I might be able to help there," Charlene said. "I know a sketch artist who works with…

"Charlene Biggar?" the nurse called out, scanning the room. "Oh, there you are. Come on back. The boys will be fine, won't you?" she asked, winking at the two young redheads.

"Yeah, Mom. We'll be good. If they're going to take pictures of her, though, call us in. We want to see her again," Carlos said.

"Yeah, huh," Chip added.

**

Mid-December

"Whoa! You sure got big in a hurry," Charlene said. "Rita, right?"

"Yeah, I did. I guess everything I eat is going to her these days. I'm sure there's only one in there, but she just hit a growth spurt. Your name's Charlene, right?"

"Yes, that's me."

"As huge as I am, I can't believe how it would be carrying twins. How big did you get with the boys?"

"I only carried one. They're not twins."

"They sure do look alike. How much age difference is there?"

"Two days," Charlene replied, then sucked in her smile before it sneaked out as a laugh.

5

"What? How can you do that? I mean, you can't have a complete pregnancy and deliver in two days!"

"I only delivered Chip. Carlos had a different birth mother. When she died, I adopted him. Actually, it was easier than that. My husband is the father to both of them so no paperwork required."

"The rat," Rita said. "I mean, I'm sure you forgave him or you two wouldn't look so happy. All's well in paradise, I hope. I haven't seen him in a while."

"He's not a rat. To put it bluntly: sperm donor. He's working or he'd be here. This is his first pregnancy. We only met a year ago. Pretty cool on the one side: he gets to be the father to the children he never got a chance to meet. On the other side, Carlos's mother was murdered. Since he could prove he was the father, no legal adoption necessary. See, you never know how things are going to work out."

"So, you have twins who aren't twins. Does it feel weird, I mean, the way you feel about Carlos compared to Chip?"

"Nope. Actually, it's pretty cool. I get to be surprised by all the little nuances that he shares with his biological half-brother. At the same time, I'm surprised by the tics and tells. You know, like the way their eyebrows raise at surprises or snorts of irritations when I serve lima beans. It's even cooler when they are shared by all three. So, are you going to rear your daughter by yourself?"

"No. Shoot, I thought by now I'd find the perfect parents for her. I even scanned through the biographies of at least fifty different couples who were looking to adopt. Anonymously, of course. Once you get on an agency's 'donor' list, they never let go. I never gave a real name and was in Seattle at the time. Oh, and please, don't say anything to the doctor, either. They usually have at least a dozen infertile women in the wings, waiting for a chance at the perfect baby."

"Any baby you get is the perfect baby. Now parents, on the other hand; those take a while to whip into shape. It's definitely a learning curve. I was a single parent for five years. My dad helped out a lot, but that was just when Chip was an infant. Do you have a job? I mean, do you have a job with flexible hours? Could you work from home? I know daycare is outrageously expensive."

"No, and no and no, I haven't taken any parenting classes." Rita looked down at her hands, folded over her bulging baby belly. "I don't hate her. I mean, she's real easy to take care of, at least now, but I'm scared. My mother was a decent person. I think she did a fairly good job with me. I mean, she was extremely upset when I told her I was a lesbian, saying that she 'blew it.' She got over that after talking with a few other parents in the same situation, though. My dad was not so understanding. I don't think I could ever go back to their house after the crap he said to me. If he saw I was pregnant, he'd never shut up about me just going through 'a phase' or some other nonsense. Nope. I'll have this little girl, give her to the right person, get my body back, and then get a life. I hope. Crap. I'm such a failure…"

"Rita," Charlene said and reached out, enveloping both the distraught woman's hand and part of her belly, "you are not a failure. Shoot! Look at you! You're building a person. And I'll bet she's absolutely perfect. And even if something didn't come out that fit the world's notion of perfect, she'd still be just how she's supposed to be. You're not drinking or doing drugs or dumb stuff like that, I hope."

"The last time I had a drink, I shared two bottles of tequila with Baby Daddy. I swore off that crap the next morning. No, before I eat or do anything, I think of how it's going to affect her. I guess in that respect, I am a good mother. Or at least, a good vessel."

"Rita Williams?" The nurse called out. "Oh, there you are. Come on back."

"See you next week, Rita," Charlene said. "I'm sure you'll find the parents you're looking for. I'm positive!"

Rita watched as the other mother-in-waiting waved and smiled in farewell. *You're right. I think I just did.*

Chapter 2: Stakeout

Surveillance is the monitoring of behavior, activities, or information for the purpose of influencing, managing or directing. This can include observation from a distance by means of electronic equipment, such asclosed-circuit television (CCTV), or interception of electronically transmitted information, such as Internet traffic. It can also include simple technical methods, such as human intelligence gathering and postal interception.

Surveillance is used by governments for intelligence gathering, prevention of crime, the protection of a process, person, group or object, or the investigation of crime. It is also used by criminal organizations to plan and commit crimes, and by businesses to gather intelligence on their competitors, suppliers or customers.

https://en.wikipedia.org/wiki/Surveillance

Mid-December

"How long is this going to take, Arlie?" Louie asked, squirming to get comfortable in the compact car's driver's seat.

"I told you the passenger seat was more comfortable," Arlie said. "Care to swap places?"

"No! Well, yeah. Maybe. My feet are either frozen or on fire. Next stakeout car you get, forget about blending in. Get something with a decent heater."

"Hey, we get what we get," Arlie said, then sipped his coffee. "Damn. Already cold. Uh, oh. They're moving…"

"Do we move in on them?" Louie asked, sitting up straight to get a better look.

"No, we're just watching." *Click, click, click.* "And taking pictures."

Louie leaned over the steering wheel and squinted. "She looks kind of familiar. What did you say her name was?"

"I didn't because I don't know her. She's been in town for a few months. She's called Tiger by those who know her. That's pretty much all we have. That and she's been hanging around with some pretty rough dudes. My guy said everyone seems to cut her a wide path, though."

"Do you think she's dirty?"

"Louie, you've been watching too many movies. I just heard there was a shipment coming into town and if we wanted to know more about it, watch where the kitty is headed. It's a longshot, but worth taking. Besides, you weren't doing anything else tonight, were you?"

"Me? No. Jess is still out of town on special assignment." Louie paused, then laughed. "Oh, I get it! Kitty is Tiger. Cool. Yeah, there she goes…"

Click, click, click.

Arlie snapped more photos, intent on following Tiger and trying for a shot of the big man who had exited the warehouse to greet her.

"Watch it!" Louie said, then held up his phone to focus on the vehicle at the other end of the dock. Its slow movement towards them was blocking the lights of the port, the only indication it was there. *Click, click, click.* "Shit!" he exclaimed and dropped his phone in the cupholder. "We're outta here."

"But…"

Before Arlie had a chance to protest, he saw what Louie had seen. The tall, all-black Jeep four-by-four with the matte-black painted 'moose bumper' was headed right at them, all lights off, the trail of vapor from the exhaust rising like a spooked cat's tail. Its bulk blocked out the lights of the harbor behind it, the variance of dark and bright indicating its stealthy stalking speed.

Vroom! Screech!

The engine roared and tires spun on the chip-strewn service road as the lifted and bloated vehicle shifted from first to third, covering the length of the hard-packed gravel drive in seconds, grit and ice spewing back, then tinkling to the ground like hail.

"Oh, man!" Louie shifted into drive and skidded around the tight corner, barely keeping all four tires of the little Corolla on the ground.

"Do you know what you're doing?" Arlie asked, the gun in his hand aimed and ready to shoot out the tires on the monster vehicle chasing them.

"No one knows The Port like I do," Louie said. "Or knows that Jeep. That's my old ride. It can climb a mountain of packed snow but can't corner worth a shit."

"Then I'm glad you're behind the wheel. Find a place to hide. They don't know if we're cops or competition at this point. Let's keep it that way."

***

"Hey, Kitty," the tall broad-shouldered man said, reaching out to embrace her. "How's my big sister doing?"

"Do not call me Kitty," she hissed, slipping out from under his attempted hug. "I'm trying to build a rep in this town. It's Tiger."

Leo the Large looked around and made sure no one was within earshot. "Two cats in one town? I guess Anchorage is big enough for both of us."

"Yeah, well it will be if you stick to keeping track of the girls and spirits going in and out of the Bush. All I care about is powdering the state. Easier to hide in fuel tanks and tires than hookers and bottles."

"You got that right. But I like sampling the goods I move more than that chemical snow. You can have that gig. I never was fond of staying up for three days straight. Plus, my dick don't work as good when I'm high."

"Not interested in your bodily functions any more now than when I was changing your crappy diapers in SeaTac. Now, tell me about the flow?"

Vroom! Screech!

"What in the hell?" Leo asked, pivoting in place, pulling his sister behind him with one hand, drawing his gun with the other.

Kitty moved away and squinted into the distance, checking out the two vehicles playing chase through the rows of stacked connexes and flatbed trailers. "Looks like a few more want to come to our party. Any idea who?" she asked.

"Nope, not really. Dozens are out for a fast buck. I figure I'll hang back and fight the winner. Let the little guys bump each other off. Fewer bullets and brass knuckles needed by me."

"You always were lazy," Kitty sneered, then punched him on the shoulder and chuckled.

"I call it being efficient," Leo said. "Come on. It's cold out here. I have a few things to show you that you might be interested in."

***

Louie let the little Toyota roll to a stop between two stacks of shipping containers, a clear exit both in front and behind him, then shut off the engine, erasing any telltale exhaust or taillight glow. "Man, that was close," he said. He flopped his head down on the steering wheel and rolled it side to side. "Sure got my heart to tickin' fast."

"Yup. Glad to see you're still living up to your nickname, Lucky. Do you know who was driving your old Jeep?"

"I sold it cheap to some Islanders. I knew they were going to flip it pretty quick and make a bundle when they did. I gave 'em a good deal just because I didn't want to mess with sellin' it before getting ghosted with the witness protection program. I figured if those big boys drove it around town for a month or so, then folks would realize it wasn't mine anymore. After that, whoever they sold it to would be safe. Or relatively safe. At least, the guys friendly to the De Lucas wouldn't be out there looking to wipe it out, thinking it was me. Li'l Boy barely fit in the driver's seat but he made it work."

"Yeah, you and Li'l Boy definitely don't look alike. I'm pretty sure he wasn't driving, though. This was a smaller person. Fair-haired and ugly." Arlie shuddered, recalling the sneer of revenge. "I couldn't tell if it was male or female — just ugly."

"Yeah, well my mama always told me, 'Ugly is as ugly does.' I guess that fits in this situation. Why were they after us? I thought we were inconspicuous in this old thing."

"I think they were after anyone in the area. Don't know if they're friend or foe to those two, but I think I'll be back out sometime after ten-thirty in the morning."

"Won't they see you?" Louie asked. "I mean, you want to come out in broad daylight?"

"You betcha. I'll be out in my puffy red vest, playing with my drone while you try to fly a kite. Unless you want to do it the other way around?"

"I'll take the kite. Me and *electronical* stuff don't get along too great. I do okay with wind and string, though."

"Cool. I'll pick you up about quarter to ten. Bundle up. It's supposed to get windy."

"Yeah, well, you bundle up, too. Glad you gave me your old Kevlar. It may be bulkier than the new stuff, but I'm pretty sure it still works."

"Only if you wear it," Arlie said. "Only if you wear it."

***

"Hey, Arlie," Louie said, scooting into the front seat of the vintage silver-toned Subaru. "I think it's cool, getting to go on ride-alongs with you and all, but I miss seeing Charlene and the boys. I hate to invite myself over, but can I come hang out this weekend?"

"Louie, we all consider you family, but I think you've been working too hard. It's already the weekend. Today is Sunday. Charlene took the boys over to Marc and Dottie's. Dottie has some great ideas for her baby's nursery. She and Charlene finagled a paint crew. My two boys and their two girls will paint while Marc supervises. The ladies are making gingerbread. When the painting is done and the mess cleaned up, they'll be assembling a whole gingerbread neighborhood, I guess."

"Ooh! Can I come? I mean, I go to the Captain Cook every winter just to see their layout of Anchorage in cookies, candies, and frosting."

"Of course, you can. It's better to drop in now — before the baby gets here — than afterward. From what Charlene tells me, it takes a long time for babies to get on a schedule. For the first few months, Mom needs to sleep when the baby does or she'll have to do without. And believe me, if it's any indication of what's going on now, she's going to be a real bear."

"Huh?"

"Charlene only has two weeks to go. The baby moves around a lot at night and keeps her awake. She said the baby's already setting her routine."

"I can come by and help. I'm really good at holding babies. I can give the baby a bottle and change her diaper. Unless it's poopy. I get nauseous when I see blood or poop."

"I'm afraid that won't work. At least the feeding part. Charlene's going to nurse the baby. You can rock her to sleep and burp her, though. Or you can take the boys sledding. They like spending time with you."

"Yeah, and I can bring back Chinese takeout for dinner, too. That means she won't have to cook as much."

"That would be nice, but remember; I'm taking at least two months of family leave. I'll be able to help, too."

"Yeah, okay. It is your baby, after all. And I'm not Charlene's real brother…" Louie said, then sighed deeply.

"Knock it off, Louie. Having one hormonal person around is enough. Your sympathy mood swings need to stop before the baby gets here or you won't be worth a darn to anyone. *Capiche?*"

"*Capiche.*"

Chapter 3: The Visit

A full moon lasts only an instant but appears to last for a day. The first full moon in December is called the cold moon. Are more babies born during a full moon? That question has been asked for centuries. According to vast amounts of data collected over the years, there is no truth to that superstition.

"Thanks for bringing me to the appointment, Louie. The boys aren't a problem, but driving isn't a good idea with a belly this big. At least, according to the doctor." Charlene flinched and arched her back as a hard contraction hit.

"Are you okay?" Louie asked. "Is the baby coming now? It's a good thing we're in the doctor's office already, huh?"

"No, she's not coming. At least, not right now. These are just warm-up contractions. Have you ever watched a dog or a cat give birth?"

"No, but I have seen women give birth in movies. They get all hot and sweaty and mean… You know, yelling at their husband, calling him names. But then they're really happy when it's all over."

"Well, most of that is true. I didn't have a husband around when Chip was born, though. I did call the man who talked me into being artificially inseminated some pretty rough names. But when I saw Chip — all slimy and wrinkly, screaming 'til his little face turned bright red — I realized it was all worth it. I was glad I did it. It'll be different this time. I have Arlie. He's promised me that not a case or crook on this earth will keep him from being with me when she's born. Missing doctor's appointments, I can handle. But being AWOL on D-Day…" Charlene's face skewed up, jaws clenched and eyes narrowed as she hissed about how mad she'd be if Arlie was a no-show.

"Whoa, Charlene. You're starting to get all mean like those women in the movies. Give him a break. He's working these extra hours so he'll be able to stay home with you when she comes along. Hey, have you figured out what you're gonna call her? I mean, we just keep calling her She. That won't work. Half the world's population already has that name."

"She?" Charlene asked, then chuckled. "Yup, half the world is female."

"I was thinking," Louie said, then paused and licked his bottom lip. "How about the name Louella? I like Louise better, but you and Arlie don't seem to care for it."

"Louie. Chill. When we see her sweet little face, I'm sure the right name will come to us. Don't sweat it. When you have a baby, you

19

can name her or him anything you want."

"Um, I don't think that's going to happen," Louie said, a blush rising. "I'm not, um, equipped that way."

Charlene glanced down at his crotch before she knew what she was doing, then shook her head. "You're a guy, right?"

"Uh-huh."

"And you haven't been castrated or kicked in the jewels and damaged?"

Louie self-consciously pulled his knees together and shook his head.

"So..."

"So..." Louie rolled his eyes, then bent over and whispered in her ear. "I think I'm gay."

"Yeah. So? Ever hear of a surrogate? Lots of guys are married and hire a woman to carry their baby or babies. Sounds like a plan. At least, after you've found Mr. Right and decide to settle down. By the way, how is Jess doing?"

"Oh, I guess it's not a secret, huh? Well, to tell you the truth, we had a spat a while back. I thought we were getting back to normal, then next thing you know, he sends me a text that he has to go deep undercover. I don't know what's really going on. I think he might be trying to dump me."

"Dump you? Pbbt! Why would anyone… Boys! Put that down. Do not feed the fish. How did you find their food anyhow?"

"It was under the tank," Carlos said. "I told him not to…"

"Hey, knock it off," Louie said. "No one likes a tattletale. Come on, let's go wash that stuff off your hand, Chip. You're coming too, Carlos."

Louie turned to Charlene. "Thanks for the pep talk. I hope you're right. We'll be back in a jiff."

"Charlene Biggar?" the nurse called into the lobby. She looked over and saw her. "Ready?" she asked.

Charlene set her hands on the wooden arms of the waiting room chair and pushed herself up. "I'm getting there," she said. "Just takes me a little longer these days."

"Before we go into the exam room," the nurse said, "the doctor wants to talk to you in his office."

Charlene followed her to the end of the hall and noticed Rita was also in the room. "Thanks," the doctor said to the nurse. "That will be all. Please shut the door on your way out."

A nervous chill ran up Charlene's back, a touch of claustrophobia at being shut in a room plus a dollop of fear at the change in routine. "Hey," she said to Rita, noticing that her fellow lady-in-waiting also looked pale.

"Hey," Rita said. "Almost Christmas. Are you and your family ready?"

"Ahem." The doctor cleared his throat then smiled at each woman in turn. "Yes, it's a busy time of year. There's a full moon in a few days. Whether it's scientifically sound or simply an old wive's tale doesn't make a difference. More babies decide to come out at the bright of the moon than not. At least, that's been my own personal experience. I never plan time off at that time of the month."

Charlene glanced from the doctor to Rita, still confused. She nodded politely and said, "So I've heard. Now, what's going on? Why am I here? Is there something wrong?"

The doctor grimaced. "No, nothing wrong." He glanced over his notes again, then looked up. "At first I thought you had birthed twins, but I see that wasn't the case. Still, Rita has come to me with a suggestion and wants me to help make it happen. You see, she doesn't want to keep this baby and wants you to have it. It would be like you have twins. I know it will be a challenge as it is for any woman taking charge of two infants at the same time. However, from what you've told me, your husband will be taking a two-month family leave and will be there to help you."

"Whoa! Wait just a minute," Charlene said, her hand up to emphasize the point. "Give me a second to process what you just said." She turned to Rita. "So, you want me to have your child? To raise her as my own? Or rather, our own with my husband?"

"I like you. I see what you've done with your sons. You seem even-tempered and financially secure. Plus, this baby will look similar to your boys. You see, the baby daddy was a redhead, too. From what I remember of high school biology, two redheads can only have a redhead, right Doc?"

The doctor nodded but didn't add to the conversation. Instead, he fiddled with his pen, shuffling the papers in front of him.

"If I did agree to this, first I would definitely have to ask my husband. I can't even begin to imagine what would be going through his head with this proposition. Second, how would we do it? Don't you think that this baby's daddy might want a voice in the decision? Maybe he wants to adopt her?"

Rita shook her head emphatically, her lips pursed tight as she fought tears. "I don't know his name or where to find him. Even if I did, he's gay. It was an accident, the two of us getting together. A drunken rage against our partners. We were mad…"

"Hey, hey, hey," Charlene said, reaching sideways to try to pull the sobbing woman close to her. She started laughing at the awkwardness. "You know what's funnier than binge-watching cat videos? Two very pregnant women trying to hug each other while sitting side-by-side in wide-bottomed chairs with arms."

Giving up on the struggle, Charlene stood up and offered her hand to the much younger Rita. "I don't know what Arlie's going to say, but regardless of whether we adopt this baby or you keep it — or by some miracle in heaven, the baby's daddy shows up — I will help you take care of her. I may not be worth a darn during delivery, depending on what's happening with my body at the time, but I will do everything humanly possible to be there for you. You and the baby are both worth it. My attention, I mean."

Rita's tears slowed down with the reassurances. "Are you sure? You don't even know anything about me."

"And yet you were willing to give me your daughter to rear as my own. Come on, Rita. Sometimes you just know something's the right thing to do, right? Helping you is right. Man, that's a lot of rights."

"Yes, you're right — one more — but I'm still willing to give her to you. That's present tense, not past tense. And I'm saying it before a witness, too. Right, Doc?"

"I have a standard form that states if something happens to you in delivery — if you become incapacitated or die — that you, Charlene, will take custody of the child. I don't anticipate any problems. You're a strong young woman, Rita, but since there isn't a father present for the child, having an alternate guardian is advisable."

"Now, that I'm fine with," Charlene said, accepting the paper from the doctor. "I'll sign that. Now, no problems, *capiche?*" she said to Rita.

"Yes, Sis," Rita replied, then attempted the near-impossible: a hug. "You're right. Our bellies are too big."

"You can owe me one." Charlene laughed and shook her head. "You know, I was born an only child, but you're the second person to claim me as a sister. Love you, both."

The doctor stood up from the desk and cleared his throat. "Enough of the legalities. Come on back and let me have a listen. You two can share a room. You may have missed it as sisters growing up, so better late than never, I guess."

Rita put one arm around Charlene and lay her head on her shoulder. "You have no idea how great this feels."

"Oh, yes, I do," Charlene replied. "The love goes both ways, Sis."

***

The women came out of the examination room, their moods even brighter than when they had entered. Charlene looked up and saw Louie and the boys on the floor, rolling their small die-cast cars into each other. "Hah!" Louie exclaimed. "The Dominator wins again!"

"You cheated!" Chip exclaimed.

"How could I? It was your car last time."

"Boys," Charlene said to Rita. "They never really grow up. I'm ready for dollies and dress-up and…" Charlene stopped when she saw the color drain from Rita's face. "Are you okay? You don't look too good."

Louie looked up and said, "Hey, Sis," then froze when he saw who was next to her. His eyes dropped to see Rita's bulging belly, then he plopped forward. Passed out cold.

"Help!" Charlene said. "You," she said to Rita, still pale and now wavering. "Go sit down. Boys, get that toy car out from under his face."

The receptionist came over to assist, rolling him over onto his back. Charlene held onto the arm of the chair as she squatted next to him, waving a magazine over his face to give him more air.

"What's wrong with Uncle Louie?" Chip asked.

"Here. This will work," Carlos said, then dumped his paper cup of water in Louie's face.

"Carlos!" Charlene hissed, pulling his hand away.

Louie sputtered and swiped his hands across his face, working to get the water out of his eyes and mouth. "What? Who?" He looked at Charlene again, then around the room. "It's you!" he squeaked. "And you're pregnant?"

"Duh," Carlos said, then he and Chip started giggling behind their hands.

"Yeah, we're only six and we can tell she's pregnant," Chip said.

Chapter 4: Full Disclosure

DNA testing is currently the most advanced and accurate technology to determine parentage. In a DNA paternity test, the result (called the 'probability of parentage) is 0% when the alleged parent is not biologically related to the child, and the probability of parentage is typically 99.99% when the alleged parent is biologically related to the child. However, while almost all individuals have a single and distinct set of genes, rare individuals, known as chimeras, have at least two different sets of genes, which can result in a false negative result if their reproductive tissue has a different genetic make-up from the tissue sampled for the test.
https://en.wikipedia.org/wiki/DNA_paternity_testing

"I think we need to take this conversation somewhere else," Charlene said as she scanned the room. All eyes were on the drama unfolding in the obstetrician's office, a mixture of smirks, scowls, and barely contained chuckles directed at the pregnant women and their families. "It would do all of us good to have some lunch, too."

No one moved or responded to her suggestion. "Get your cars, boys," Charlene said, her mommy voice strong and without room for protest. "We're going to splurge on fish and a salad bar. I think all of us could use a little brain food."

Rita remained mute, her eyes wide as she stared at Louie, who was trying not to look at her. Still on the floor, he reached over to help pick up the toy cars, stealing glances at his one and only heterosexual encounter: a one-night-stand. He started to swoon again when he saw how huge her belly was. She was as big, if not bigger, than Charlene. His mind raced as he tried to count backward. *How many months ago was it that he and Jess had their first big spat? Had his breakup revenge sex resulted in a baby?*

"Rita, you're coming with us. For some reason, I don't think I trust you to make it to the Sea Kitchen on your own. Louie's driving." Charlene took the reluctant woman's elbow and tugged, urging her out the door.

"I think I know the name of your baby daddy," she whispered so only Rita could hear.

"Is it that obvious?" Rita whispered back, then chuckled nervously.

A quick snort of a laugh escaped from Charlene. "You couldn't have picked a greater guy, even if you had planned it." She looked back at the boys, urging Louie to hurry up. "Move it, guys. It's a sad day when two pregnant women can walk faster than three young men."

"Hey, Mom," Carlos called out once they were all buckled in and the car was rolling. "Can Uncle Louie put in Alice Cooper? I want to hear 'School's Out.'"

"Who lets you listen to that?" Charlene asked, then frowned at Louie.

"Hey," he said, defending himself. "School *is* out 'cause it's Christmas vacation. Plus that song's on my mixtape. I made sure there weren't any explicit songs on it."

"Oh, all right," Charlene said. She looked over and saw a slight smile appear on Rita's face. She nudged her and whispered, "Told ya."

Rita slowly shook her head with a pleased acknowledgment, her grin continuing. "I must have seen something there, right?"

"Yeah, he's a keeper."

A scowl overtook the smile as uncertainty sprang back with a vengeance. "Not for me."

Charlene patted Rita's hand that was resting on the only place available to a nine-month pregnant woman in the back of a minivan: her belly. "I'm not asking for anything but for you two to get to know each other. No romance required or expected. All right?"

"Not a problem since I'm not drinking. The no romance part, I mean. Being sober definitely means there won't be any hide the sausage games going on. As far as getting to know him… We'll see."

"Well, no matter what, you did say you wanted me to rear your daughter as my own, right? Or did that change?"

"Yes and no. I mean, yes, I still feel the same way. No, I'm not changing my mind. I'm just in shock, all right?"

"Just making sure. As you'll see, Louie is a part of our life. He's the other one who claimed me as a sister. Whether he's in her life as her uncle or her daddy, he'll be there for her. Eerie, huh?"

"Yeah. Huh," Rita said, then twitched as the baby kicked.

Louie pulled up to the handicapped space in front of the restaurant, then leaned sideways to retrieve the white and blue placard from the door's side pocket. "I guess one sign will work for two pregnant women?" he joked, his nervousness showing in the squeak when he first spoke.

"As long as we're in one car, only one hangtag needed," Charlene said. "But I know I'd like a hand getting out. And I'm sure Rita would, too."

"Rita," Louie said softly, then walked around her side of the car. "Hi, Rita. Nice to see you again," he said.

"You, too. Louie," she replied, her voice stilted. She looked over at the boys, trying to help their mother exit the minivan. "I'm fine, but I think your sister might need a hand."

"Oh, yeah. Hey, guys. Let me get your mom out. Why don't you hang with Rita and escort her in?"

Carlos took Rita's hand as Chip raced ahead to open the door. Just as he pulled the door completely open, he looked up. "Daddy's here!" he hollered. Chip leaned forward, ready to run to his father, then remembered his job and stepped back. "See! I'm helping," he said, standing at attention in doorman position as his father strolled in from the parking lot.

"That's my boy," Arlie said. "Hey, Carlos. Do you need a hand?" He looked up at the pregnant woman he recognized from Charlene's obstetrician visits and greeted her. "Hi, I'm Arlie. I don't think we've been introduced."

"Rita," she said, accepting his stronger, steadier hand to assist her over the salt and gravel-sprinkled parking lot. "That's the only bad thing about the temperature warming up; more ice."

"You got that right. And, from what my wife tells me, your center of gravity literally shifts minute to minute, second to second."

"Yup. This one's a regular acrobat," Rita said, then stole a glance over to Louie.

"Hey, I took gymnastics when I was a kid! I was a really good tumbler. I could do flips and everything," he said, then blanched. He looked down at his hands and started counting backward again. "Oh, man…"

Charlene moved past Louie who was still looking down, studying

32

his fingers as they incessantly tapped one another, counting and recounting, hoping he had made a mistake. "Keep coming to the same conclusion there, Louie?"

"Yeah. I think I'm going to be a daddy," he mumbled. His once pale and stunned face suddenly brightened. "I'm going to be a daddy!" he announced proudly to anyone and everyone in the waiting area.

"Really?" Arlie asked, looking from Louie to Charlene then all around the room, searching for whatever clue had just been dropped that he had missed. "When?" He asked, then leaned next to Louie and asked, "And who."

"You can't be a daddy," Chip said. "You're not even married."

Carlos nudged Chip. "You don't need a piece of paper to have babies. Cows and dogs have babies all the time and they're not married."

"Oh, yeah. Huh."

"Let's see," the silver-haired waitress said. "How about we get you seated back here? There's more room. Plus, I don't think you'll want a booth today. Maybe in a month or so, right?"

"How'd you guess?" Rita asked.

"Five of my own plus six grandkids. All girls. Get comfortable while I go get some kids' menus and crayons for the boys."

Out of habit, Arlie arranged his family where they would be safest and he'd see everyone coming in. "Hey, Louie, why don't you sit over here? Carlos, you sit between Louie and Rita. No. Wait. You need to be on the outside so you don't bump everyone."

"I can eat with my right hand, too," Carlos said, then reached across to grab a packet of saltines. "See," he said, trying to pull the tear strip on the packet with his non-dominant hand. "Oops. I guess this one's opener is broken."

"Don't worry about it, bud. I don't want you flipping clam chowder over everyone here. Come on, switch places with Louie."

Louie stood up and changed places, now seated next to the blushing mother-to-be. "Hey," he said to her, his face radiant with his new status of father-to-be.

Arlie looked over at the couple entering their section of the dining room. "Oh, no," he said softly and quickly grabbed a menu. He sat down, only his eyes visible as he followed the couple sitting down two tables away.

Louie turned back, saw what Arlie had seen, and repeated, "Oh, no."

"What?" Charlene and Rita asked, looking back, too.

Rita gasped, then leaned into Louie's shoulder. "Hide me," she said, her voice shaking with fear.

Not wasting a moment to ask why, Louie put his arm around the baby mama's shoulder and held her close, his face pressed into her hair. "I got you. Both of you," he said.

"Thanks," Rita said, sniffing. "It's her."

"Okay." Louie resisted the urge to turn around and look but did glance up and saw Arlie's steely features. Gone was the perky dad taking time off in the middle of the day to have lunch with his family. Here was the undercover cop studying the man and woman he had been stalking for a week.

Louie's brain tumbled emotions and scenarios over and over. Cool. Now he and Arlie knew one of Leo and Tiger's hangouts. Not cool. Arlie was here with his family. If Leo the Large and Tiger got busted then released on bail, it was possible they might remember seeing Arlie and his family. His fraternal and paternal protection instincts started taking over and a guttural growl slipped out. They'd know Charlene and her distinctive redheaded boys on sight.

His fears subsided. Unless Leo or Tiger already knew Arlie, the undercover cop wouldn't stand out — they wouldn't have a reason to remember him. Besides, this was only one of the scores of restaurants in Anchorage. His family was safe. Suddenly Louie's nose tickled, bringing him out of his family worries and concerns.

His family concerns? Last year, he had no one other than the fake family he had tried so hard to be a part of as a child. Now he had two families, one of them was biological, the first since his mother had been killed. He snuggled the mother of his child closer. "I got you, Rita. You don't have to worry about anyone as long as I'm around."

Rita twisted free and looked into his eyes, not even trying to conceal her doubt and mistrust. "And how long are you going to be around?"

"Um. I'm not going anywhere. How about you?"

Rita grimaced and shrugged a shoulder, but stayed mute. Leave no clues.

"So, how'd you know we were going to be here for lunch, Arlie?" Charlene asked, hoping to warm up the awkward situation.

Eyes directed towards his wife, but focusing on Leo the Large and Tiger, Arlie nodded to her cellphone on the table. "Checked out any good apps lately?" he asked and chuckled.

"Duh!" she whispered. She opened up her tracking app and saw the two icons, side-by-side.

"Yeah, if only keeping track of bad guys was as easy. The two who just came in are the two Louie and I have been watching for a while." Arlie turned his attention back to his sons. "Hey, guys. How about letting Uncle Louie take you back to wash your hands?"

"But we just did that at the doctor's office," Chip said. "We got fish food all over 'em."

"Speak for yourself," Carlos said. "I didn't get fish food on mine."

"Wash your hands now," Charlene said using her no-nonsense voice. "No explanations or excuses."

"Yes, Mom," they chorused, then bounced out of their seats to follow Louie.

Rita kept her eyes focused out the window in front of her. She didn't want to turn around and look. Besides, where she was now, she could catch glimpses of her former girlfriend in the window's reflection when a big truck drove by. She let out an unintentional deep sigh of longing. The woman who had suddenly disappeared and broken her heart nine months earlier was less than fifty feet away.

After several minutes of awkward introspection, Rita asked, "Where is the ladies' restroom?"

"Behind me," Arlie said. Seeing her discomfort, he added, "Don't worry. They won't see you unless they're looking for you. Charlene, why don't you go with her?"

"Really?" she asked, wondering why he would send her off to visit the john like she was a child. Then she saw the worry in his eyes. "You're right. If I don't go now, I'll probably get the urge as soon as the food gets here. I'll take a salad and clam chowder if the waitress comes back before we do."

"Ditto," Rita said. "And an iced tea."

***

"So, what's going on?" Charlene asked once they were in the restroom.

Rita rushed into the handicapped stall and locked the door. "It's her," she said, then sat down to pee and cry. "Damned pregnancy hormones," she sobbed. "Everything is worse by a factor of five, at least."

"Yes," Charlene agreed from the stall next to her. "But the good stuff is bigger and better, too."

"Wouldn't know. I haven't had any good stuff happen to me in ages."

"Well, then let's just hope it will all catch up to you soon. You have us in your life now."

"Yeah, well, knowing my daughter is going to have a good family to watch over her did give me a cool little tingle."

"Aha! You do claim her. You called her *my daughter*. Have you figured out a name yet?"

"No. I figured you'd want to do that since I'm just the birth mother and you're going to be her real mother." Rita started sniffing again. "Can we not talk about it now?"

Flush.

"Sure. I guess this is a face-to-face conversation, not a toilet stall-to-toilet stall one."

Charlene washed her hands and waited for Rita to compose herself, checking for wayward hairs in the mirror.

Thunk.

The restroom door opened and the woman who had given Rita, Arlie, and Louie the shivers walked in. The handle on the handicapped stall jiggled at the same time; Rita was ready to come out. Charlene reached up and held the door closed at the top. "Make sure you wipe, honey," she said to Rita, then looked up at the woman who had spooked everyone. "Cold out there today," she said, hoping her voice sounded casual and not shocked.

"Yeah, it is," the woman replied in a low, throaty tone. "Then again, it is December in Alaska."

"Yeah, well, there is that."

Rita recognized her former girlfriend's voice and backed away from struggling with the door. She could — and would — wait.

Click, click.

Hearing the other stall door lock, Rita tried to open her door again, this time feeling no resistance. She stepped out, looked around, and only saw Charlene.

Charlene had the water turned on for her, a paper towel ready. Rita gave her hands a fast scrub under the running water, then quickly dried them. "Thanks," she whispered and led the way out the door.

"She's pretty," Charlene said once they were clear.

"Yeah. I forgot how much she scared me, though," Rita said.

"But I thought she was your girlfriend."

"She was. Very much past tense. More later," she said when she saw everyone at the table watching them come closer. "Maybe."

"You look wonderful," Louie said, standing up to hold her chair for her.

"I feel as big as a trailer house. With tip-outs!"

He let her scoot in by herself, hoping he wasn't being too forward. "You're positively radiant, but you probably hear that all the time."

Rita giggled, then quickly stifled what she was afraid sounded like a flirt. "No, actually that's the first time anyone has said that to me."

"Well, then you're just not hanging out with very observant people because I'm sure you've always been this lovely." Louie paused, suddenly insecure. "I'm not being too forward, am I?"

"Cool! Crayons!" Carlos hollered, accepting the cup and printed out kid's menus from the waitress. "Do you want one, too, Louie?" he asked.

Louie looked embarrassed at the gesture and shook his head. "Not this time. You go ahead and color mine."

"Is everyone ready to order?" the waitress asked, then said, "Oh, wait. I have something for you." She reached under her work apron and pulled out a small plastic baggie with a shot glass in it. "This was hers," she whispered to Arlie.

"Thanks," he said and slipped it into Charlene's purse.

Charlene looked up. "Leda?" she asked, then saw the name tag read Dale.

"Well, it would be if you flipped the letters around," the perky senior said, then winked. "Nice seeing you again, Mrs. Biggar. Looks like all's going well with you and the baby."

"Yeah, it is," Charlene said, slightly stunned. "And welcome back out of retirement." Charlene glanced at Arlie, still perusing his menu. Yes, he was aware that his former Middle Eastern Studies teacher was working undercover. She was probably his eyes in Midtown, keeping track of some of the same people he was watching. The clever woman had helped her out of a hostage situation a few months ago. She was an asset wherever she was. Charlene looked up and said, "I'd like a bowl of clam chowder and a dinner salad. No, make that a trip to the salad bar and a cup of chowder."

"That sounds good," Rita said. "I'll take the same."

"Me, too," Louie said, his eyes twinkling in delight. *I'm going to be a daddy!*

"Boys?" the waitress asked.

"Um…" they mused as they scribbled on their menus, intent on their paper canvases.

"They'll share an order of fish and chips," Charlene said. "Add a couple of bucks to the price of my 'all you can eat' salad. I'll make them a plate of fresh fruit and veggies to go with the fish."

"Got it. And you, sir?" Leda asked.

Arlie set his thumb on top of the menu he was offering her. He looked her in the eye, then down at his thumbnail and over to the table where Leo and Tiger were seated. He winked and nodded. "I'll have the same as the other big kids," he said.

Leda deftly slipped the miniature microphone from his thumbnail into the crook between her thumb and base of her forefinger. "Anything to drink, sir?"

"Just water. And water for the boys, too. I don't want them cranked up on sugar."

"Except me," Louie said. "I want a cola…" He caught the glare from Charlene. "I mean, I'd like an iced tea, too, please."

Charlene's scowl quickly segued into a smile. "That's my baby brother. Such a good role model for his nephews."

"So, you two aren't related at all?" Rita asked Louie. "I mean, it looks to me like she has your number as if she's been in your life forever."

"Nope. It's only been about a year now. Arlie, too. We're all kinda newlyweds that way. I mean, we didn't get married as a family. She and Arlie did, though, about a year ago. Carlos came into the family at about the same time. Hey! That's right!" Louie looked around the table. "We have an anniversary coming up."

Arlie caught Louie's eye and shook his head, warning him not to bring attention to the family. "Oh, yeah," Louie said, much lower. "I think it's a few weeks away. Let's see if we can plan something special for it."

"I'll let you do the planning, Louie," Charlene said. "I think I'm going to have my hands full."

"Huh?"

"Baby," she said. "Remember?"

"Babies?" Rita added, insecure at being in the midst of such an endearing family but wanting her new friend to remember her commitment.

"Oh, yeah! Me, too!" Louie said in a hoarse whisper. "I think I'd better watch some videos on how to take care of babies. I never thought I'd have one."

Sniff. Sniff.

Louie turned to the young woman next to him as she tried to hide her unbidden tears. "It's okay. I'll take care of both you and the baby." He hugged her across the shoulders, eager to protect them both. "I have a job and everything. My apartment's small, but I can get a bigger one."

Rita's back tensed at the unfamiliar gesture, a man's touch. Her stomach churned at the thought of losing her independence. "I can't," she said. She started to stand up, then heard it, and sat back down. That low, throaty laugh. *Kitty*. Seductive yet cruel. How had she let herself fall in love with someone like that?

"We'll see," Rita said to Louie. *Yes, we'll see how long after this baby is born that I find a way to leave Alaska and get back to where I belong. They're depending on me.*

Chapter 5: Cat Scratch Fever

Sibling rivalry is the jealousy, competition, and fighting between brothers and sisters. It is virtually inevitable if a parent has more than one child. Problems often start right after the birth of the second child although it sometimes starts before the baby is born. This competition and/or animosity occurs between siblings whether blood-related or not.

"Why Alaska?" Kitty asked.

Leo grabbed the last beer-batter halibut chunk and swiped the remaining smear of tartar sauce from the cup with it. "You know, Alaska, the Last Frontier? Not as much competition, either. Everyone's huddled inside, trying to stay warm."

"Bullshit," she called on him, then held up her shot glass and waited for the waitress to come back. She caught her eye. "Another Cuervo Gold."

Wiping cloth still in hand, the silver-haired waitress took it with a smile. "Coming up," she said. She looked at the big man, then down at the empty plate. "More fish?"

"Yeah, sure. Why not? The ocean's still full of them. I guess I can help with the harvest." He looked back at his sister. "So, I thought you never wanted to see me again. What happened with that?"

"Got tired of the same old scenery. Too much rain in Washington. Figured Alaska needed more 'snow,'" she said and added a menacing smirk.

Leo looked around the room, then realized it was safe from eavesdroppers. No cops or competition that he could see, just a couple of guys, their pregnant wives and two redheaded brats. This restaurant was a decent enough place to handle business, plus they had good eats. "So, how much are you gonna give me for letting you work my contacts?"

"What do you think is fair?" she asked, then laughed ominously. "Let me know, then maybe I'll give you half that."

"Still the greedy bitch," he said. "Come on, where's my snack? I'm hungry."

"Still the gluttonous bastard," she retorted. "If it's not a tapeworm, you must have a tape-*serpent*."

"Nah, it just takes a lot to keep this high metabolism running fine."

"Here you go, sir," Leda said, setting the plate of halibut down in front of Leo. "And for you," and put the shot of tequila on the coaster. "Are you ready to order?"

"Yeah, bring me your biggest t-bone, rare. You know what I mean. Just get the chill off it. And bring me two potatoes. One of them baked and loaded and the other twice-baked. And how about you surprise me with one of those craft beers everyone's always talking about? I'd like to change up my usual lunch just a little."

"And for you?" Leda asked the woman, unsure if she would be offended with the designation of 'Ma'am' but certain that calling her 'Miss' would feel awkward for both of them.

"Just a dinner salad with oil and vinegar on the side," she said. She dipped her finger in the tequila and rubbed it around the rim of the glass, trying to make the glass sing like a crystal goblet.

"Wrong kind of cup," Leo said. He dipped a piece of the fish in the sauce, held it up to her, and bellowed, "Cheers!"

"Wrong kind of toast," she said, then continued messing with her drink, hoping her intel had been right. Sometimes getting close to someone in order to take over was just too easy.

***

"Hey, Dad," Carlos asked. "Would you do us a favor? Since Duffy can't be Santa Claus this year at the Senior Center, would you play him?"

Arlie looked from Charlene to Louie, and then back to his son. They both shrugged shoulders. *We didn't tell them; how do they know there isn't a Santa?* "What are you talking about, 'play' Santa?"

"Dad, we're almost seven now," Chip said. "We know that Santa can't be everywhere before Christmas. He's too busy building last-minute toys, scheduling delivery routes on his GPS, checking the naughty list twice, and all that stuff. He hires out…"

"Or gets volunteers," Carlos continued, "to play him at events like schools and malls and those kinda places. So, since Duffy got a new hip and won't be back from pre-fab or whatever that place is called…"

"Rehab?" Charlene asked.

"Oh, yeah, that's it," Carlos said. "He'll be at the rehab place for at least another week. So, would you be Santa? I know it would mean a lot to the seniors…"

"Yeah, they're all excited about seeing Santa. They won't recognize you, especially with the fake beard and all." Chip paused, his face skewed up as he thought hard. "I think we'll have to use all the pillows from home to stuff in the Santa uniform, though. Duffy's pretty big and never needed padding. You're kinda skinny. You'd look funny if we didn't put something in there."

"You couldn't get that fat even if you ate cookies and pie for the next three days straight!" Carlos declared.

"Yeah," Louie added, "But it'd sure be fun to try, huh?"

"Come on, guys," Charlene said, breaking up the chitchat before

48

Arlie would have to confirm or back out of the commitment. "It's time for the salad bar. Let's go see what kind of fruits and veggies they have."

As soon as Rita started to back away from the table, Louie was on his feet, helping her up. "Here, allow me," he said, his face radiant.

Rita couldn't help but grin and shook her head. "I sure didn't see this one coming when I woke up this morning."

"Yeah," Louie muttered. "Me neither." He cleared his throat and spoke up clearly, "I mean, never in a million years did I ever think I would be a daddy."

Rita's grin disappeared. "We need to talk." The boys rushed past her on the way to the salad bar. "But later."

"Oh, yeah. Later, for sure."

Charlene dished up carrot sticks and melon slices for the boys. "Take these back and get started on them," she said, then lingered, waiting for a chance to talk to Rita in private. "Psst," she whispered, trying to catch her attention.

Rita's lips pursed as she looked at the bounty before her. She had been on a very limited budget for months. Fresh fruits, vegetables, and fish were definitely out of her price range. The baby turned over again, reminding her that her stomach capacity was limited and she shouldn't be greedy. Suddenly, she felt Louie's absence. He'd been in her life for less than an hour but a void opened up as he left for the table without her. She looked around and saw Charlene trying to get her attention. "Yes?" she asked.

"Hey, how about coming to my place after lunch? I want to make sure you're comfortable with our, ahem, arrangement before I bring it up to Arlie. I mean, just in case you don't like our neighborhood or you think the house is too small, or…"

"Sure. After lunch will be fine. At some point, though, I'll have to get a ride back to my apartment or a bus stop. And it's not the size of the home but the love of the family. You and your husband and sons will be perfect, I'm sure," Rita said, glad that tears hadn't sprung up this time.

"And don't forget her uncle or daddy or whatever Louie's going to be. I mean, he does have a say in this, too."

"Oh, yeah. That does complicate things, doesn't it?"

"Only on the legal level. My dad's a judge which means he knows the law. I'll have him check into it."

"Wow!" Rita added asparagus spears and giant green olives to the bed of romaine, spinach, and baby greens. "Your life seems so convenient."

"Wasn't always. Well, except for the dad part. I was a single mom for a long time. An interesting story for another day, but all I'm trying to say is don't discount anything as impossible."

Rita set her plate back down on the bar and put a hand on Charlene's shoulder. "I'm not going into this lightly. I've been wondering about you for a couple of months, ever since I saw the way you worked with your two sons. They'll be an asset helping with the girls, I'm sure. Uncle or Daddy Louie will be a bonus, too. One thing I will promise you, though, is once you've accepted her into your family, I'll never try to take her back. I might want to pop in for a visit when I'm back in the state, but I won't 'claim' her, all right?"

Charlene nodded and smiled nervously. She'd never thought of that. "We both have to have faith that we'll do the right thing."

"Amen to that," Rita said. "Come on. I want to see if I can eat all this and still have room for the chowder."

"Eyes are definitely larger than stomachs on pregnant women. We can always have the chowder to go and fill up on fruits and salad while we're here."

"Never thought of that," Rita said.

"I'm full of surprises. Stick around and see."

"I'll trust you on that." *Because I'm not going to stick around.*

Louie pulled out the chair for Rita, then saw that Arlie was intent on his phone and hadn't risen to help Charlene. He moved over and got the chair for her, too, looking down at whatever app Arlie was mesmerized with. Nothing. Literally, nothing was on his screen. "Are you okay, Arlie?"

Arlie looked up, gave a half-hearted grin of embarrassment, then tapped his right ear.

"Oh, yeah," Louie said softly, realizing that even though they were at lunch with family, Arlie was multitasking, working a case, eavesdropping on Leo and Tiger. "Don't worry," he whispered. "I'll cover for you."

Arlie shook his head minimally, then realized the women had returned from the salad bar and were already eating. "Oh, sorry 'bout that. I get a little distracted sometimes. I'd better get my chewable vitamins and minerals before the brain soup comes in."

"Ew! Brain soup," Carlos said.

"Cool! What's brain soup?" Chip asked.

"Fish is supposed to be good for your brain," Charlene said.

"Yeah, I didn't get to eat any fish except canned tuna when I was growing up," Louie said. "Just think how smart I'd be if we had fresh halibut and salmon around — real brain food."

Rita patted Louie on the shoulder. "I'm sure you're plenty smart. At least, smart enough to become part of this family."

Louie looked over at Carlos who was listening in on the conversation, his eyes narrowed at the man who had once claimed to be his biological half-brother and had tormented him every time they were near each other. His face relaxed and he smiled, remembering the whole story he only found out about when he was in kindergarten. "Yeah, Louie used to be my brother a long time ago, like when I was real little. He was mean to me but that was so I'd scream for my mom — my first mama, the one who had me, the one who's in heaven now — so the bad guys wouldn't hurt me."

Carlos saw the shock on Rita's face. "See, he was protecting me even though I wasn't his real brother. He was a good guy even when he was pretending to be a bad guy."

Louie dipped his head in embarrassment. "She doesn't need to know everything," he said softly.

"No, I don't, but it sounds like this is a very interesting family."

"Yeah, it is, Rita. I'm really glad you're hanging out with us," Carlos said. "Would you come to Christmas dinner, too? I'm sure it'd be okay with Mom. We always have lots of food and open one present on Christmas Eve. Hey! You can spend the night, too, so you can be there with us on Christmas morning. Dad always makes a great big breakfast because we won't eat lunch until afternoon. I can sleep on the couch and you can have the bottom bunk."

Louie leaned in. "She can have the guest room. I'll sleep on the couch. We don't want you going outside and getting lost when you sleepwalk at night…"

"Oh, yeah. Huh."

"Is everyone ready for the main course?" Leda asked, looking around, her eyes stopping at Arlie.

He looked up, blinked once, then announced to everyone, "Oh, yeah. We're good to go. Let's chow down, then I have to get back to work. Louie, thanks for taking Charlene to her doctor's appointment. These long hours are rough, but they're going to be worth it to get two months off."

"I hope so," Charlene said, then groaned as the baby kicked. "I think she's tired of her confined space. I swear she's trying to punch her way out."

Rita suddenly sat up straight. "I know *exactly* what you mean."

"Almost twins," Louie mused, a serene smile on his face.

"Again," Charlene thought. "Maybe."

***

"We're home! Can I open the door, Mom?" Chip called out.

"Hey, it's my turn," Carlos whined.

"What day is it?" Charlene asked.

"Monday," groaned Chip and backed away to let Carlos push in the security code.

Charlene turned to Rita. "On Sundays, Arlie or I enter the code. The boys alternate the other days of the week."

"Yeah, a lot less arguing that way," Louie said. "Charlene and Arlie are really good at negotiating conflict, huh?"

"I try my best," Charlene said. "Come on in. There's a bathroom on your left just after we get in. I'll take the one in my bedroom."

"Cool," Rita said. "You read my mind."

"Nope. I'm just very sympathetic with your condition. This is great, having someone who truly understands what's going on."

"Can I start a fire?" Louie asked, standing by the gas fireplace.

"Sure. Watch him, boys," Charlene joked. "Don't let him add any wood."

"Hey! That was only one time and it was the first time I'd been here."

Rita came out of the bathroom to a roaring fire, the mantle above the huge fireplace lined with stockings: Mom, Dad, Chip, Carlos, Louie, Baby. As she looked around to scope out where she should sit, Louie looked over at her. "Hey, why don't you sit here? If you sit on the couch, you might never get up. The rocking chair's for Charlene, but we can get another one. This is the biggest living room in Chugiak, I think."

"No, Louie, it's not," Charlene said. "But it's just right for us. Did you want to take a look around first? That takes less energy than sitting down and getting back up again."

"Ah, spoken like someone who's been there, done that," Rita replied, her hand on her hip as she stretched the muscles in her back.

"Still there, still trying to work through that. Okay, so over here is the kitchen, back here is the guest room," Charlene held the door open and let her look in, but could tell that Rita wasn't interested in that room. "The boys' rooms are upstairs as is the spare room, but I'm sure you'll want to see this." She opened the door to the master bedroom and headed right to the walk-in closet. "*Voila!* I always said it was bigger than Chip's room when he was a baby."

Rita followed her through the bedroom and looked into the closet. "Oh, it's beautiful," she cooed, the tears welling up in her eyes. "A full-sized crib even."

"Yeah, well, I wasn't sure if I was going to use a co-sleeper or not. All I had for Chip when he was little was a dresser drawer. That worked until he got bigger, then I got a playpen and I used that. Of course, he normally slept with me since I was single and had a queen-sized bed."

Rita fingered one of the many soft cotton sleeping gowns hung in a row, various shades and prints of pink and apricot with a few aqua and yellow on either side, a veritable rainbow display of clothing.

"My dad's new wife — I have a hard time thinking of or calling her my mother — went a little overboard with shopping."

Rita beamed at the warmth and wholesomeness of the new home her baby would be coming into. "Yes, I'd say you definitely are set up for two daughters. The crib will fit both of them for a while, too."

"You're sure you want to do this?" Charlene asked.

"More now than ever. All you have to do is make sure Arlie is willing to take on another one."

"I really don't think that's going to be an issue. A year ago, he didn't have any children. I mean, biologically he did, but he didn't even know there was a second one. When Carlos's mother died, it wasn't even a question of whether or not he would take on the responsibility. What the big question is going to be is what about Louie."

"Louie is not a question," Rita said harshly, then took a deep breath and softened her tone. "I mean, before I even knew he was in your life, I wanted you as the mother. The real mother. I'm just the birth vessel. He was just the sperm donor."

"Hey! I resent that!" Louie said, stepping forward.

Suddenly claustrophobic, Charlene's hands started waving everyone away. "Out! Out! I can't breathe."

Louie and Rita both stepped back, watching as Charlene rushed to the outside door, exiting and closing it behind her.

"See what you did?" Rita hissed.

"Me? You called me 'Just the sperm donor.' I'm more than that. Or can be. I mean, I didn't make a baby on purpose. Shoot! We were both drunk, but we still have a daughter together. I want to be a part of her life. I mean, I *am* her daddy."

"No, you're her father. I want Arlie to be her daddy."

"You give her to Charlene and you won't have a say in it."

"Oh, yes I will!" Rita huffed, then heard the boys clamoring in the living room, setting up the race track for their toy cars.

Wanting to reassure her, Louie reached out to put a hand on Rita's shoulder. Seeing her flinch, he stuck it in his front pocket instead. "You love this baby, and so do I. You've had nine months, more or less, to figure out what you want to do with your life and hers. I've had about two hours. Give me a break. I'm not a rotten guy. No matter what, this baby is going to be loved. Yes, I'll need Charlene to help me, and Arlie will be a big part of her life, too. But I want to be her daddy.

"I see Arlie with the boys and a big part of me gets jealous. Hell, all of me is jealous. I never thought I'd have the chance to have a child. I was over the top excited when Charlene said she was pregnant. I knew right away she was having a girl and you know why? Because I always wanted a daughter. Her baby — Arlie's baby — was going to be the closest I'd ever get to a daughter. Don't take that away from me. I haven't done anything wrong. I haven't hurt you. Shoot, I didn't even know your name." Louie scratched his head, thinking. "I don't think I ever told you my name, either."

"Yes, I didn't know your name, either. I kinda wondered if it was Jess because that's what you kept calling out when we were, you know…"

"Making a baby?"

Rita giggled and blushed. "Yeah, we were making a baby. I know I was drunk but I really needed you at that time. I was so blasted mad at my girlfriend for ditching me. And then, to make matters worse, I saw her at lunch today."

Louie looked side-to-side. "When. Oh, you said lunch. Where? You mean that woman drinking shots and picking at her salad with that big dude who was eating enough for a village?"

"Yeah, that was Kitty."

"Oh, yeah. Now I remember that name. I think that's what you were calling me."

"Probably. She's a skank. I'm glad she's out of my life." Rita shuddered. "No telling what she'd do if she saw me pregnant. Not that it makes a difference. Whatever it was she wanted out of me, she must have got it. She was all over me one day, then gone. Split. Not even a good-bye text or forwarding address for the crap she left at my place."

"Oh, man. We gotta tell Arlie about this," Louie said, his face pale. "Hey, how'd you know she was here? I mean, did you follow her to Alaska to try to hook up with her again or something?"

"Well, kinda sorta. I wrote angry letters to her at her old address, letting her know what a tool she was. Of course, she never replied. I don't even know if she ever got them. But then four months ago, I got one returned to me with a yellow forwarding address sticker on it that said, 'This forwarding address has expired,' or something like that. It was a PO Box in Anchorage. So, yeah, I kinda followed her up here. I guess part of me wanted to tell her off, another part of me hoped she'd see my big belly and want to raise a child together, especially after I found out I was having a girl.

"Then, I saw Charlene and Arlie at my doctor's appointment. I never said anything to either of them the first time. The next time, Charlene and I started talking. You know, waiting room stuff. When are you due? Are you having a boy or a girl? By then I was sure I didn't want to be a part of Kitty's life, no matter what. I was too far along to do anything about the pregnancy..."

"You wouldn't!" Louie blurted before he could think.

Rita patted her belly. "Obviously, I didn't. I couldn't. When it was just a missed period then morning sickness, I considered it. I didn't have the money…" She paused, her face scrunching up as she did some soul searching. "I guess I could have if I sold everything I had because that's what I wound up doing: selling everything so I could come up here, looking for Kitty. But no, once this little one started fluttering around, I knew she was real. She may not be for me, but she was perfect for someone else."

"Like me?" Louie asked hopefully.

The scowl returned. "I really didn't think about you. No offense, but my opinion of men is pretty low. I mean, what man in his right mind would want to raise the child of a one-night stand?"

"Me." Louie paused, really thinking about what she had said. "I think you'd be surprised. Yes, it would be a shock to a guy, especially if he didn't know the chick or was involved with someone else, but…"

Louie's legs faltered. His hand reached out to hold onto the wall. "Hey!" Rita said. "I think you'd better sit down. You don't look too good."

"Oh…man…" Louie let her lead him to the rocking chair in Charlene's bedroom.

"Oh, man what?" Rita asked. "Are you all right?"

He shook his head and cleared his throat, hoping for clarity, then got it. "This is my child," he declared. "And if Jess and I are to go forward in our relationship, he's going to have to understand that she's a big part of it. Scratch that. She's all of my life now. She's my reason for living, working, bettering myself…"

"All right, all right," Rita said. "I think I understand your dilemma." She huffed to compose herself. "Never saw this coming," she said softly.

"Like I said, you've had nine months to prepare." Louie looked at his watch. "I've had almost three hours now. So, what do you and Char have going?"

"Just a verbal before a witness: our doctor, and a paper that says if I kick the bucket, the baby's hers."

"So, you'll let Charlene and Arlie and me work it out?" he asked hopefully, his hands tucked under his chin as if praying.

"Yeah, that'll work for me. No matter what, I know she's going to be loved. If she winds up with two dads, that's cool. At least, I know she'll have a loving mother and two adoring big brothers."

"Hey! And they'll look alike, too!" Louie said, his sparkle and *joie de vivre* returning. "Since we both have red hair, she will, too!"

"Are you always this optimistic?" Rita asked.

"Yup! And she will be, too." Louie stood up and reached for her

62

hand. "Come on. Let's go make sure nothing's happened to Charlene. I want to make sure she didn't slip on the ice or something. Arlie would clobber me if I didn't watch out for her."

***

"Here you go, sir," Leda said, setting a full-sized to-go box in front of Leo. "On the house for being such a good customer."

Leo popped the lid up and smiled. "A piece of death-by-chocolate cake. My favorite. Shoot, Dale," he said, looking at her name tag to make sure he had it right, "you know I'd leave you a big tip no matter what. Thanks for putting it in a to-go box, too. I am a bit full."

Tiger aka Kitty rolled her eyes, then pushed away from the table. "Come on, little brother. Time to get to work."

Leo handed Leda three one-hundred-dollar bills. "See you tomorrow!"

The waitress folded the bills around the tab and stuck it into her apron pocket. "Make sure you save that dessert for later. I wouldn't want you to get a bellyache."

"Me?" Leo asked, then laughed out loud, patting his ample gut. "Never."

Chapter 6: Waterworks

Births and Natality for USA 2017
Number of births: 3,855,500
Birth rate: 11.8 per 1,000 population
Fertility rate: 60.3 births per 1,000 women aged 15-44
Percent born low birthweight: 8.3%
Percent born preterm: 9.9%
Percent unmarried: 39.8%
Mean age at first birth: 26.
https://www.cdc.gov/nchs/fastats/births.htm

"I'm back," Charlene said. "I just needed some fresh air. You two were in there a while. Did you get everything worked out?"

"Yes," Louie said at the same time as Rita said, "No."

"Sorta," they said together, then looked at each other and grinned.

"Well, compromise is good as long as everyone's happy," Charlene said.

"We agreed that you are the mom. You both seem to think Arlie's flexible. The three of you can work out the dad situation," Rita said.

"Except I'm the daddy, for sure. We'll have to figure out all the rest. It's okay to have two dads. I know it is because lots of kids have more than one mom or one dad. Sometimes parents divorce and remarry, then there's a stepmom or stepdad or two. And sometimes they don't even have to be divorced. Remember Mac? He had two dads at the same time, under the same roof."

Charlene rolled her eyes. "Yes, you already spend a lot of time here, Louie, but I don't know if I'm ready for you to move in full time."

"Uncle Louie's moving in?" Carlos asked.

"Yeah, all the time?" Chip added hopefully.

"Hey, never say never," Louie said. "Your guest room is about the same size as my studio apartment. I'll pay rent and everything."

"Ugh…" Charlene sighed. "Let's wait until your father comes home to talk about it," she said, putting a hand on each son's shoulder. "This is definitely a two-parent decision."

"Three-parent," Louie said brightly. "Because pretty quick, I'm going to be a daddy, too."

"Uh, yeah, real soon," Rita said, moving away from the kitchen stool she'd been sitting on. "I think my water just broke."

"Oh…" Louie moaned and started to swoon.

"Knock it off, Louie," Charlene said and pushed him in the shoulder to get him to stand up straight. "Breathe. I'm gonna need help here, and picking you up off the ground is beyond my physical abilities right now."

Chip came over and looked down at the floor at Rita's feet. "I don't see any puddles."

"Go to your room, boys," Charlene said. "Now! I'll be in there in a minute." She shuffled them off, then said, "I hope."

"I took the initiative and grabbed a fistful of paper towels," Rita said. "Doc told me to stay put and not to move if it happened, but I gotta tell you, all I want right now is to jump in the shower. This feels so icky."

"You got paper towels?" Louie asked, looking around. "I don't see any paper towels."

"Grr." Rita looked down at the bulge in the crotch of her maternity slacks where she was holding the impromptu diaper together with her thighs.

"Oh. Oh…" he moaned and started to swoon again.

"Louie, we don't have time for this." Charlene grabbed a kitchen towel and ran it under the faucet, then briefly squeezed it out and slapped it on his neck. "Arlie's working undercover. I know he is. He was doing his thing at lunch. What are the chances of him breaking loose right away?"

Louie shook his head, using the ends of the towel to wipe his face. "Slim to none. He's been following Tiger and Leo for a few days. My guess is that when he saw them going to the same place we were having lunch, he popped in to make sure you and the boys were all right."

"Tiger? You mean Kitty?" Rita asked. "And aren't we supposed to be on our way to the hospital?"

Charlene shook her head. "We're okay for a while. Or you are. I think. As long as you're not hemorrhaging you're still at the waiting stage. She'll need to be delivered within twenty-four hours, though. Your labor will be starting pretty soon. Or should."

"So, what am I supposed to do?" Louie asked, pivoting in place, the prime example of a nervous father. He looked in the refrigerator. "No sodas?"

"No, no sodas. There's leftover coffee, though, if you're looking for some quick energy. It's pretty good iced, so help yourself." Charlene turned to Rita. "I'm making this up as I go along. I'm not supposed to drive. Louie can do that. But, you're going to need — or most likely want — a birthing coach. I can do that while Louie watches the kids. Dottie is out of town until tomorrow, so I don't have my last-minute sitter."

"Hey! I want to be there when my daughter's born. I feel fine now. Maybe we can do like the wrestlers do."

"Huh?" Rita and Charlene asked.

"You know, tag team. You go in for a while, help her out while I

67

watch the boys, and then switch out. But when it's time, I want to be there when my little girl comes into the world. Nothing's gonna stop me from being there for her."

Sniff, sniff.

Charlene put her arm around Rita's shoulder. "Yup, I guess my little girl is going to have two daddies."

"And an aunt who pops in for a visit every year or two?"

"Or as often as she likes. Go ahead and park your butt back on the stool. I have to put together a to-go bag for the boys. Oh, and you can use mine. I can repack it after you're done delivering."

***

Once they were on the road, Charlene cleared her throat to get everyone's attention. "All right, listen up. One. I called the doctor to let him know what's going on. Two. I left a message for Arlie, so he'll know where we are. Three. I've got the tablets loaded with books and games for the boys…"

"Did you get mine?" Louie asked.

"Uh, no. You're going to be busy with other stuff. Besides, you have your phone."

"Oh, yeah. Cool! I'm gonna take lots of pictures of her. Would you snap one of me when she sees me for the first time, Char?"

Sniff, sniff. Rita's sniffles of emotion quickly transitioned into rages as a sudden and unexpected pang of discomfort hit. "Oh, shi…take! Shitake, shitake, shitake!!"

Chip and Carlos laughed, then brought it down to a snigger behind their hands at seeing their mother's glare. She turned her frown of reprimand into one of concern as she looked at Rita. "Are you all right?"

Rita shook her head, then nodded, paused, finally blurting in frustration, "It hurts!"

"Don't forget to breathe," Louie called back over his shoulder. "I mean, that's what they always say in the movies."

"He's right," Charlene said. "Did you ever take the child-birthing class?"

"No. I didn't have anyone to be the coach. Plus, it cost money. I barely had enough to cover rent, food, and bus fare."

"Hey, after she's born, what are you going to do?" Louie asked. "I mean, we can share the same room at Charlene and Arlie's if you want. I mean, I'm sure…"

Rita didn't say a word, but when Louie looked into the rearview mirror to continue the conversation, he saw words weren't needed. "Okay. I'll shut up. We can talk about it later. That is if you want to."

"Smart man," Charlene said.

Huff, puff, huff, huff. "Argh!"

"She sounds like a pirate choo-choo train," Chip said, then giggled.

"Hush, guys," Charlene said.

"But I didn't say nuthin'," Carlos said.

"And now you just did. I never thought I'd hear myself say it, but get back to your tablets, boys. I think it's going to be a long day."

Sniff, sniff.

Charlene reached back and patted Rita's leg. "Don't worry, dear. No matter what, she'll be out by tomorrow at this time."

Every muscle and bone in Rita's body went limp at the remark. She had been in such a hurry to get rid of the pregnancy. Now that it was almost time, the feeling of loss drained her. This situation had been such an inconvenience: she had given up her job — her career, her passion— and lost her lover… Scratch that; the lover would have been split no matter what. She shook her head as another pang hit, then gave into it. She let it roll over her like a chilly breeze on an otherwise balmy day. These last spasms, no matter how painful, were all she had left of her daughter. She'd cherish them.

***

"Don't worry about finding a parking spot, Louie. Just pull up in

70

front and get valet parking."

"Hey, Mom," Carlos asked after they were out of the van. "Is Rita going to be okay? She looks kinda pale and sweaty."

"She'll be fine. And even if there's a problem, we're in the right spot for someone to fix her up. Now, you two stay with me. Let Uncle Louie take her up to the desk. We're going to hang out here in the waiting room for a while."

"Is she going to have the baby today?" Chip asked.

"She'll have the baby sometime today or tomorrow for sure. Get comfortable, because we might be hanging out in here for a long time."

"All set?" the nurse asked Rita as Louie pushed the wheelchair to the admitting desk.

"Yeah, I preregistered a month ago," Rita said, then clenched her jaws and took slow and easy breaths. *You're still mine, little one.*

"And are you the father?" the clerk asked Louie.

"Yes, I am," he said proudly. She handed him an ID badge with DAD and his name printed on it. He hung it around his neck, then looked over at Charlene and the boys, waiting in the lobby. "Oh, but I'm only the part-time coach. My sister's the one who's doing most of the helping there. I didn't get to take the classes, so we're tag-teaming it. You know, like the wrestlers? Besides, someone has to

71

stay with the boys. They're my nephews. We're tag-teaming them, too. I mean, not bringing them in to see the baby being born…"

"You're babbling," Rita said, gritting her teeth.

"Oh, yeah. Right. Where to now?" he asked the clerk.

"Here's Sonny now. He'll take you both back. Good luck!"

"We'll need it," Rita said softly, tears now streaming down her face.

***

Bwap!

"Don't you have any control over your bodily noises?" Tiger asked Leo. "And who eats that much at once without getting sick? I can't believe you ate that chocolate suicide cake already, too."

"It was death-by-chocolate. And hey, what can I say? It was free."

"Yeah, but you ate it in the car. While driving! It looks like the inside of a dumpster in here. Why don't you have it detailed, or at least power washed out?" Tiger picked up the empty cake container from the dash and tossed it behind the seat with the mountain of other bags and food containers. "You had better set up rat traps in here or you'll wind up bitten."

"Don't you know they don't have rats in this port? Or anywhere else in Alaska, I think."

"That's only because they haven't found your truck yet. When they do, there'll be a population explosion." She shuddered at the thought, then kicked up the heater to high. "Now, where's this contact you said would help me?"

"For a price," Leo said. "A price for him and for me. Are you sure you want to get into the meth business? The competition is pretty rough up here. Everyone wants to get a piece of the action because it looks so easy. It isn't. Why do you think I stayed away?"

"I don't know or care what you're afraid of," Tiger said, then took off her scarf and set it on top of his cellphone on the seat between them. She pointed out the window to a high rise with a series of boarded-up windows, inching the bundle closer to her at the same time. "What's going on there? It looks too new to have issues."

"Don't know, don't care," he said. "We're almost there. Put on your iron skivvies. These dudes are bad."

Tiger pulled the scarf the rest of the way towards her and slipped his phone into her coat pocket. After taking a long moment to bundle up, she took a deep breath, watching the two big men exit the lifted black Jeep. "On second thought, I think Alaska's too cold for me. Take me back to my hotel. I'm packing up and going back to Seattle."

"What? Those two scare you? Are you a scaredy-cat, Kitty?"

"Shut up, Leo the Lard," she hissed. "And don't ever call me that again or you'll be sorry."

"Ooh," Leo said, then didn't make another sound. He'd heard that hiss and knew to respect it. You didn't want to mess with Kitty when she was mad. Tiger really should have been her birth name.

Leo rolled to a stop in front of the hotel, set the truck in park, and was about to get out and open the door for her when she stopped him. "I got this." She pulled the latch and held onto the door handle, sliding down the side of the leather seat until her boots hit the ground. She slammed the door shut then smacked it, giving him the all-clear and sending him on his way. "Thanks for everything," she said and waved.

She turned toward the hotel entrance, stuck her hand in her pocket and felt her prize. "Yes, thank you very much for everything."

***

'Did U get freq?' Leda typed in.

'A-OK,' he typed back. 'Thx.' Arlie changed screens and watched the blip stop at the port, then backtrack to a hotel downtown. It paused, then went back to the port. "Looks like someone didn't want to stick around," he said. "I'd say there's a division in the ranks, whether Leo knows it or not."

Ping! Ping!

"Hey, Louie, what's going on? Charlene didn't go into labor, did she?" he asked, suddenly terrified.

"No, she didn't but her friend Rita did. I'm gonna be a daddy! And real quick. But hey, I got that covered. Or we do. Sorta. I gotta tell you something really important before things get crazy here with Rita being in labor and all. That gal Tiger that we've been watching? Yeah, well, her real name's Kitty. Or at least that's what Rita called her. They were girlfriends a while back, before I knocked her up. Rita, not Kitty. Anyhow, Rita said Kitty was after something when they were dating. She's pretty sure Kitty only pretended to like her so she could get information out of her. She doesn't know what it was, whether it was names or dates or what. Oh. Okay. You can come down and try and talk to her but I don't know if that's going to do any good. She's… *Ouch!* Hey, Arlie. I gotta go. She's squeezing my hand so hard, I think she broke it."

Click.

Arlie looked up at the clouds, thinking about what he had just heard. "Kitty and Tiger, the same person? Yup, sounds logical. Sounds like a trip to the hospital is coming up."

***

"Shit! Where's my phone now? Damn." Leo fumbled through the trash on the seat, then looked behind him and swerved, almost hitting a pedestrian. "Damn! Okay, time to clean out the truck."

Forty-five minutes and three filled trash bags later, Leo gave up and admitted to himself that his second suspicion was right. Kitty had taken his phone filled with contacts. "Damn! Damn! Damn!"

He jumped back in his truck and drove in a reckless rage back to his apartment. The tires screeched to a skidded stop, hitting the concrete barrier, preventing him from rolling into the apartment's living room. "Damn! Damn! Damn!" he repeated, his mantra the only thing keeping him from smashing a door, a wall, or an innocent bystander.

Once inside, he logged into his computer and hit the 'find my phone' app. 'No device is attached to this app. To set up, please…' Leo shut the laptop and leaned back into the plush leather couch. Time for plan B. Go right to the big guy and do a joint venture. He'd bluffed his way into rougher situations. It was time to get back in top mental shape. No family guilt trips allowed. His thieving big sister had conned him again.

Chapter 7: Any Port Will Do

Slavery never ended – its name just changed...its new name: human trafficking.

The modern slave trade is a 150 Billion Dollar industry and an estimated 30 million people are currently enslaved. Of this group,2 million are child sex slaves. Crime organizations are attracted to slavery because a child can be sold over and over again — drugs can just be sold once. As cold as this sounds, it makes economic sense if you don't see the value of another human being.

https://medium.com/@erikcbrown267/operation-underground-railroad-the-modern-day-abolitionists-

O.U.R: Operation Underground Railroad, started in 2013 by Tim Ballard, is a group of former CIA agents, special forces soldiers, and law enforcement who travel the world trying to end child sex slavery. Its success includes making sure those rescued get aftercare: the assistance to help recover from the trauma, indignities, and brainwashing they endured. More information at https://ourrescue.org/

"Are you sure they're here?" she asked, peering into the back of the long silver shipping container,

"Oh, yeah. Check this out." The broad-shouldered man with the dark knit cap pulled down tight over his ears aimed his keychain flashlight into the back of the refrigerated produce trailer. "Supper time!" he bellowed.

Tiger watched as a single row of boxes slowly shifted forward, the boxes of packaged fresh broccoli moving toward her like the rows of animated cells in a video game. Pensively, a Native American female no more than twelve years old came forward, her jaw jutted out in determination, eyes squinted at the bright light she was walking toward. Another young woman followed, her hand gentle on the young leader's shoulder. "Water?" the second one asked, her voice squeaky from dehydration.

"Yeah, sure. Why not?" Hero said. "Stay put a sec." He looked over at Tiger, then down at the bulge in her jacket. "Make sure no one tries to split. I gotta get them somethin' to drink."

The man who claimed the name Hero lifted the back of his down jacket and tucked his pistol into his insulated snow pants. He walked around his matte-black Jeep and pulled a case of water bottles from the back. Digging around, he found a carton of granola bars and threw it on top, then brought the bundle to the half-opened door of the semi-trailer. He reached up and set it down on the floor and shoved it in. "Hey, you! Short stuff! Spread these around. Dinner and a drink. No charge. Your last meal in Alaska. Cheer up, ladies and gents. Didn't all of you say you wanted a free ride Outside?" He ended his snide dissertation with a raucous laugh that sent shivers up Tiger's already chilled spine.

"Will they make it?" Tiger asked. "Doesn't it take a long time to go south?"

"Only four to five days on the steamer," Hero said. "They got honey buckets in there plus all the broccoli they can eat. This container's insulated so they shouldn't freeze to death. At least the ones we shipped south in October didn't. They don't have a clue what's up. I told 'em I was making a movie. They were gonna be extras. The best-behaved ones — the ones who showed me and the guys 'extra favors' — were gonna be the stars in the show. The ride might be rough, but I told them they were building character — making them into more believable actors."

"Are they all Natives? I could have sworn I saw a blonde head back there."

"Nah. All I cared about was that they were young, especially if they had something special going on like different colored eyes or a midget or something. The big guy down south said his clients were after unique kids. I told him I had a line on something that'd make his clients' dicks real hard: Eskimo girls." Hero rubbed his crotch. "Works for me every time. My own little freezer full of Eskimo pies…"

Tiger groaned at his lame joke and pulled her jacket closer. "Would you hurry up and shut that can? It's cold out here. Let's either go to your office or get back in the Jeep to conclude our business. I'm not used to this shit. I'm ready to go back to Mexico."

"Whatever you want, Kitty."

Tiger reached out and grabbed him by the throat. She squeezed his voice box hard, waiting until his face turned purple-red before she spoke. "Don't ever call me that again. My name is Tiger. Got it?"

Hero nodded, no breath to speak or even cough.

She released her grip and stepped back as if nothing had happened. She looked up. The two young women had been watching. They blinked, their fixated stares broken, then ran through the narrow pathway of boxes, into the front of the trailer. Tiger glanced back at the coughing and sputtering Hero. "Looks like they're already slightly seasoned. Won't take long until they're prime. They are bare, right? No branding or tattoos?"

"I thought about doing it but that wouldn't work. At least, until they were corralled. Now that I have them penned, you can do whatever you want. They ain't going nowhere. You're not doing nothing to them until I get paid, though." He stood up, grabbed his gun, and aimed it at her in one quick, smooth move. "Got it? 'Cause I don't care how strong your grip is or who you're related to, these chickens are mine. I went out and gathered them, found the trailer, paid off the port agent, and got the shipping docs in order. This trailer is cleared to go to Tacoma tonight. I don't care if it's you or Leo.

Either way, cash only."

"How about a little business opportunity?" Kitty said, nonplussed at the gun in her face. "I hadn't planned to go this route — live goods, that is. I have my cash tied up in this." She pulled her designer bag out of the passenger side of the Jeep, unzipped it, and took out a baggie of white powder. "I prefer to deal in only the finest. The purer the product, the less bulk to move. You can cut this shit three times and still have prime stuff. You take this off my hands and in exchange, I'll take this sweet little ride down the Al-Can," she patted the side of the Jeep, "and meet the chickens when they get to Tacoma. All I need to do is get the goods to my place in SeaTac, then I'm ready to start distributing."

Hero put his gun back in his waistband and accepted the package of white. He pulled back the tape covering the slit in the top, dipped his pinkie in the powder, and sampled it. "Whoa. You're right."

He took a deep breath, glanced at the size of the tote bag on the seat, then looked down the length of the forty-foot long trailer. "Yeah, this shit will be a lot easier to move. Just don't forget to buy more water for them. That case will only last them a day or two. You don't want to make landfall with dead bodies. Even the stink of broccoli won't cover the stench of corpses if someone does pop in for a surprise inspection."

"Papers?" Tiger asked, her hand out. "And do you have a rig on standby, ready to transport this once it gets to port?"

"The trucker's just waiting for my call. Hand me that bag and we'll call it a done deal."

"Lock it up first and give me the key," she said, her eyes narrowed in suspicion. "And I'll get my own trucker." She glanced over her shoulder, feeling the presence of someone else. "And tell your little buddy over there in the shadows that I don't like being spied on."

Hero looked back to see if she was bluffing or not. He caught sight of the reflection of the yard lights on his guy's glasses. "She's cool," he called back. "Meet you at the spot."

Vroom!

Tiger waited a moment until she heard the big-engined vehicle leave, then handed Hero the bag.

Pop! Pop! "Idiot," she said, then kicked him over.

"But we had a deal," he moaned, grasping his gut.

"And now a few minor points have changed. I'm giving you a break. You'll live. Probably. Climb into my car and drive away. Never look back, never say a word. Find some sweet, rich old broad and live off her until she kicks the bucket. A lot safer than dealing drugs and running chickens."

Hero tucked in his knees and elbows and struggled to stand up, begrudgingly accepting her hand to help him stumble over to her rental car. He stopped before getting into the driver's seat. He looked into her eyes, trying to see if she was going to shoot him again but saw nothing. He was a bloody mess that she didn't want to deal with. It was easier for her if he drove away than to deal with a dead body at the back of her trailer of goods. Soon, forklifts would be teaming through the yard, picking up trailers and connexes, loading them onto the steamer for the trip south. Yes, she'd let him leave and dispose of his own bloody body. He slid into the seat as she held the door open for him. *Burn in hell, bitch! I hope they catch you.*

***

Shipping Office, Port of Anchorage

"Do you think you can help me out?"

Li'l Boy shook his head, pretending to say no but knowing his smiling eyes and broad grin would give him away. "You know I'd do anything for you, Arlie. There's nothing illegal going on around here, though. Nope. You don't have no probable cause, so no way you'd get a warrant."

"But," Arlie prompted, knowing that the former juvenile delinquent still had a soft spot for him. No one else had been willing to stand up for him when he made a dumb mistake as a teenager. His adult record was sparkling clean.

"But being a good guy is the gift that keeps on giving, right, Arlie? Or something like that. What are you interested in tonight?" Li'l Boy looked around. "What? You didn't bring your buddy's canine friend with you to help sniff around?"

"Nope, just me and that itchy, crawly feeling that something isn't right. Can I look over your manifests?"

"Sure. Do you want the paper copies or want me to share a digital file with you?"

"You can do that?" Arlie asked, then added, "Legally?"

Li'l Boy shrugged a shoulder. "You're not the only one with app skills, Arlie. I have a few, too."

"Let me look over the paper ones first. If I need to dig deeper, I'll let you know."

Arlie accepted the tattered plastic notebook bloated with barely legible duplicate copies. Sitting down at the lunch table, he scanned through them, turning pages one by one, looking at the cargo manifests. His mind started to wander, thinking about how little time he had until Charlene was due. Three days away by the calendar, but any time by a woman's biology.

He was beating himself up with guilt and almost missed it. He went back two pages. "Broccoli? Who in the hell ships broccoli out of Alaska in December? Nah. Something's wrong here. Hey, Li'l Boy. Can you help me out on this one? Where is this trailer?"

"You gonna let me go undercover with you?" Li'l Boy asked. "I can act all innocent and stuff. Plus, I got my concealed carry permit." He opened up his polyester vest and showed off his holstered Glock. "Cool, huh?"

"Yeah. Let's hope you never have to use it. You can consider yourself undercover if you'd like, but you're not on any payroll or duty sheet. You're undercover undercover; just a dock worker, helping me locate a missing container. Hmm. A forty-foot reefer unit full of broccoli. Does something seem a little odd to you? What can you tell me about it?"

Li'l Boy scanned the paperwork and shook his head. "Someone else took this in, not me. What? Where in the hell is all this broccoli coming from? They harvested everything in the valley months ago. I don't think broccoli keeps that long, even under refrigeration."

"Tell me where the trailer is and I'll see what I can find."

"You need an escort to go snooping around," Li'l Boy said. "Hey, Randy," he called out. "I'm gonna take my break. Catch any phone calls, will ya?"

"No worries."

"Okay, Arlie, let's go. The cart's all charged up and ready to roll.

It's brand new; electric so no one will hear us coming."

***

Crunch. Crunch. Crunch.

"Well, it may have a quiet motor, but there's no way to quiet these icy roads."

"Wait a sec," Arlie said, his hand up to tell Li'l Boy to stop. He nodded to a spot of activity directly ahead. "Is that where we're going?"

"Yeah, it is. What are they doing out here? This is a restricted area."

"Cut your lights and hang back. I think I recognize that Jeep."

"Shit ya! That was mine!" Li'l Boy hissed in a harsh whisper. "Hey," he squinted into the darkness, trying to discern something. "They painted it. It's still black, but not shiny. It's matte black so it doesn't reflect light. It's a stealth machine — a four-wheel-drive urban monster rig. Your sixth sense is still working, Arlie." The big Pacific Islander patted the gun in his vest. "I got your back."

"Don't even think about it. I'm not engaging anyone. No warrant. No probable clause. Just an itching suspicion. I don't care how good my record is, shipping broccoli out of Alaska in December is not a reason for a warrant."

"Hey, Arlie. It looks like someone's getting away," Li'l Boy whispered.

Arlie watched for a second. The driving was erratic, overcorrections on turns and intermittent speed and clumsy attempts at braking. "Don't worry about that one. He won't get past downtown before he's stopped for drunk driving. He or she's been shot but won't make it past Sixth Avenue."

"Yeah, I guess you're right. Shouldn't you call for back up?"

"For what? I still don't have anything. Just hush a minute and let me watch."

The two of them watched as the woman rummaged through the contents of the back of the Jeep, finally discovering a two-liter bottle of brown soda. She twisted off the cap and sprinkled the contents over the ground in front of her, apparently trying to cover or dissolve whatever was at her feet, then tossed the bottle aside. Her back suddenly straightened and she looked around.

Someone's watching me. I can feel the eyes on me. Well, Mister Cop, how about I draw you out?

Tiger held a gun to her head as if to shoot herself. She wailed out loud in feigned agony. "I can't go on like this anymore!"

"Arlie, we gotta do something," Li'l Boy said, then pushed the lever forward and headed to intercept what he perceived as an attempt at suicide.

"No!" Arlie gasped, grabbing Li'l Boy's forearm, but it was too late.

"Why, hello my little friends," Tiger said. "Been watching me long?"

"Hey," Li'l Boy said, his eyes squinted in confusion. "You weren't going to hurt yourself, were you?"

"Me? Nope. Never. But I am looking for a couple of heroes. I had one, but he just drove off. He had an injury and had to take himself to the hospital. Come on, dipwads. Open up this door and climb inside."

Li'l Boy stood up, but Arlie remained seated.

"You're a cop, aren't you? Don't care for anyone telling you what to do. Well, I don't either. How about you save your little friend's life by leading the way?"

"Huh?" Li'l Boy asked before thinking.

"If he doesn't do as I say," Tiger said, "then I'm going to shoot *you*."

"Come on, Arlie. Getting shot would really ruin my Christmas," Li'l Boy said.

Arlie gritted his teeth, angry at himself for letting his compassion get in the way. Not with the apparent suicide — he had seen right through that one — but with letting a civilian get in harm's way.

"Your gun, sir," Tiger asked snidely, hand out.

Arlie reached inside his vest and handed her his service revolver.

"And your other gun?" she prompted.

Arlie lifted an eyebrow, ready to play dumb, then saw her sheer hatred of his kind. He put his leg up on the edge of the electric scooter and handed her his ankle piece. "Satisfied?"

"Not really. I'm sure you have knives and whatnot stuffed in various places, but they won't bother me once you're inside. Climb in. You first, then the big boy."

Damn! So much for Plan B! She's sure to shoot both of us once we're inside.

"Hey, Li'l Boy," Arlie said, making sure the scared big man made eye contact with him. "It's okay," he assured him. "She doesn't want to shoot us. We're just going south. Didn't you say this container was going to Tacoma?"

"Uh-huh," he answered, head nodding, eyes blinking back tears of fear.

"By the time we get there, she'll be long gone. It looks to me like she already has what she wants. Right?" he asked Tiger, pointing to the bag slung over her shoulder.

"Yeah, sure. Whatever you say, Copper. You know everything. Now scoot inside or I'll shoot this kid and drag his carcass behind my new ride. Lots of ditches to dump him into."

Arlie grabbed onto the handrail on the back of the van and climbed inside. He blinked, trying to adjust to the darkness, and noticed a gap in the rows of boxes that appeared to be an aisle. "Give me your hand and I'll help you up," he said, squatting down, arm out to the terrified longshoreman.

Li'l Boy's eyes went side-to-side, wondering what Arlie was up to. He wouldn't give up this easily, would he? This woman reeked of evil. Normally, he wasn't afraid of anything, but this dark-haired witch spooked him big time. Foot on the first step, then the second, Li'l Boy reached out and accepted the wiry redhead's bare hand. Suddenly, he felt his three-hundred-pound body lurch forward as the detective half his size pulled him into the trailer with one hand, his other grabbing the concealed Glock.

Arlie stepped aside — letting the big man crash harmlessly into the stack of boxed vegetables — and fired at the steely-eyed heartless thug.

"Shit!" Tiger growled, the bullet burning as it pierced her right shoulder. Still, she managed to squeeze off a shot. She missed both of them, her aim compromised by the shock of being wounded.

The big Pacific Islander quickly pushed through the boxes and scrambled to his feet. "Watch out!" he screamed, trying to pull Arlie back to safety.

Tiger switched the gun to her left hand and fired off two more shots — *Pop! Pop!*— then sneered as both men collapsed in a heap of blood and cold-weather gear. "Dumb cop and stupid concerned citizen. I hope you bleed out before you hit the water." She awkwardly unzipped her vest with her left hand and stuffed her right hand into it, creating a temporary sling.

"Damn it all. This is certainly not how I expected this to go." She pulled the snow shovel out of the back of the Jeep and used it to shove the big man's arm back into the trailer. Grunting with the extra effort needed, the wounded assailant still managed to slam the door shut and secure it. "Bon voyage, dummies."

Chapter 8: D Day

New research data from a federal study by the NIH (National Institute of Health), comparing almost 140,000 births, shows that average labor time was longer in the early 2000s than it was in the 1960s (when most labor patterns were recorded).
It has been reported that it takes the typical first-time mom 6.5 hours to give birth nowadays, while about 50 years ago, first-time moms labored for less than 4 hours. Researchers attributed this difference to a variety of factors, including maternal age has increased: At the time of giving birth, the mothers in the year 2000 were on average about four years older than the women who gave birth in the 1960s. The study researchers cite that older mothers tend to take longer to give birth than younger mothers.
https://www.verywellfamily.com/length-of-labor-how-long-will-it-be-2759011

Providence Hospital, Anchorage.
December 21

"Is she going to be okay?" Louie asked the nurse who had stepped in to check on her. "I mean, is this how it is for all women? Can't you do something for the pain? She's not asking for anything, I know, but I'm hurting for her." Louie kissed the back of his fingers, then groaned. "Well, part of me really *is* hurting. That gal has a grip!"

"No!" Rita hissed, then went back to puffing and panting like the labor room nurse had shown her. When the contraction and breathing routine was over, Rita elbowed her way up higher.

"Here, let me help," Louie said. "Hey, you're doing great. I can hear some of those other women down the hall. One of them is yelling and cursing at her husband – or boyfriend, maybe – just like in the movies. Can I get you a cup of ice or a washcloth or something?"

Rita shook her head slowly, staring at the table in front of her, underneath the TV that was on but muted. Louie had bought her flowers when Charlene had come in to spell him. He'd only taken enough time to down a soda, use the bathroom, and get her a gift. Why couldn't she find a woman that kind and thoughtful?

"Here," Louie said, his hand opened flat. "Maybe this will help. One of the nurses said if you suck on a peppermint, your mouth won't feel so dry."

"My breath's that bad?" she asked, a smile of gratitude slipping out. She took the wrapped candy, then just as she popped it in her mouth, another contraction hit. "Oh, crap."

"Yeah, oh crap. Here we go again," Louie said. He lay his hand back on the bed next to hers. He had found out early in her labor to be literally at hand but not intrusive. If she needed or wanted to grab onto something, she would. Like labor, like life. He'd be there for her when she was ready.

Hoo! Hoo! Hoo! Hoo!

Rita finished her breathing routine then sunk into the pillows, tears spilling from her eyes. She hurt more than she ever had, at least physically, but these tears were different. It was like they were prompted by a chemical reaction.

"May I?" Louie asked, a moist washcloth in hand. "Looks like you need a little freshening up."

"Are you always this nice?"

"Um. Yeah, pretty much. I mean, if you're nice to me, then I'll be nice to you. Or even if you're not. I mean, you're having my baby," he babbled, uncomfortable with the left-handed compliment. "But even if you weren't or it was someone else's baby, I'd help you,"

"Why?"

"Um," Louie took a moment to deep think his answer. "I guess it's because you need help and I'm here. Wouldn't you help me if I was hurting?"

"Sure. I mean, yeah, sure — go ahead and spruce me up a little."

Louie blotted her face gently, then offered her the cup with ice chips. "I'd ask if you'd like anything else, but I don't think you can have anything. At least now. The nurse said it's almost time."

Hoo! Hoo! Hoo! Hoo!

"I got ya," Louie whispered, this time taking her hand. He needed her right now whether she needed him or not.

"Phew! That was a tough one. Yes, I'd help you if you needed it. I guess I'm the same way. That was my job before I got involved with Kitty. I used to help people in need. Most of them were young women, but there were a few guys who got caught up in the mess on the street. Shoot, I barely made enough to live on, but I'd still do it, even if I had to work another job just to be able to afford to work with the kids."

Louie picked up her hand and kissed it. "I knew you were a good person. I mean, after we met the second time. I wasn't looking for a good person that first time we got together. Actually, I wasn't looking for anyone. I was just looking for a bottle."

"Don't get all melancholy on me now, Louie."

"I'm not. I'm just saying that I really truly deep down to my tailbone or liver or whatever, believe that there's a reason we're both here right now. Don't you feel it, too?"

Where's a contraction when I need one?

"Are you all right? I mean, except for the labor thing. You look a little green. Do you need the bedpan?"

Rita nodded frantically, the bile burning the back of her throat.

Louie grabbed the semi-U shaped container and held it under her chin with one hand, supporting her back with the other. A strong contraction hit just as Rita spewed green puke.

Louie squeezed his eyes tight and held his breath, doing everything he could not to contribute to the vomit mess on the bedding and sleeve of his shirt. He opened one eye to check on Rita, and realized that she wasn't making her huffing and puffing noises. "Breathe!" he ordered, then held his breath and shut his eyes again.

Hoo! Hoo! Hoo! Hoo! Phew! "Oh, God. I think I'm gonna die."

"Not an option," Louie said. He set the pan on the tray table, then reached up and pressed the nurse call button. "We have a situation in here," he said.

A very long minute later, the nurse was in the room. She saw the mess and didn't even ask. She grabbed a fresh gown from the closet and did a quick and discreet change of gowns for Rita. "Here are some wipes for you. There's a bag for soiled clothes in the top drawer. You might want to take off your flannel and stick with the tee-shirt. Didn't anyone get you a gown?"

"No, ma'am. All I got was the name tag." Louie looked over at Rita and saw the same green glow. "She's gonna be sick again…"

The nurse reached behind her and grabbed the bedpan. "This'll work in a pinch," she said. Rita cleared her stomach again, this time two people helping support her back. "I hope you're ready, Dad, because once mom's cleared her tummy, it usually means she's ready to deliver."

Turning her attention back to Rita, she poured a cup of water and said, "Rinse and spit, but don't swallow."

Rita obeyed, then another contraction hit. "Oh, no…"

"I'm going to check you," the nurse said, quickly putting on her glove and bending to look between Rita's knees.

"I'll leave," Louie said, having been dismissed by Rita on all previous occasions.

"No!" Rita blurted out, then continued huffing and blowing.

"Okay," he said meekly, then sat back down and picked up her hand.

"Well, she's crowned. I'm calling for the doctor. Don't go anywhere, either of you," the nurse joked, then shucked her glove and rushed out of the room.

Her hand now clutching his rather than the other way around, Louie bent to kiss hers. "I'm so proud of you."

The tears had returned to her face. He reached for the washcloth but she shook her head and brought their coupled hands to her cheek. She kissed his hand tenderly. "I couldn't have picked a better father if I'd been looking. I know I said you, Charlene, and Arlie could work out the parenting together, but I vote for you for daddy."

Louie started sniffling, his tears falling. "Yeah, I vote for me, too."

"Do I have time to glove up?" the doctor asked.

"Can I use the bedpan first?" Rita asked. "I gotta go poop."

"Okay, I'll take that as not too late," the doctor said. "Mom, that's just the baby pressing on those nerves. She'll be here in a minute or less…and here we go."

Hoo! Hoo! Hoo! Hoo! Shit! Shit! Shit!

"Good girl. Keep breathing. Yes, go ahead and push. Now relax until the next contraction." He looked at Rita. "I'm sorry, but I didn't get a chance to look at your chart again. If I remember right, this your first child, correct?"

Rita nodded, then another contraction hit. "Not again," she grunted, then started huffing and blowing.

"Almost there," the doctor said. "Now relax. The reason I ask is you're doing fantastic for a first-timer."

"Really? You mean it's usually worse than this?" she asked, letting her shoulders relax into the pillows and Louie's forearms.

"Next time you have a baby, make sure you come in as soon as the contractions hit. You've only been here a few hours, right?"

She nodded again, then leaned forward, grabbing the back of her knees and pushing without being prompted.

"You got this, Rita," Louie said.

"And here she is," the doctor said. "Relax a sec. Breathe."

Louie watched as the doctor bent to work, his neck and shoulders shifting as he maneuvered the baby out. Then he heard the squeal. "Is that her? Can I see her?"

Rita started giggling. "I sure hope it's her. I don't think anyone else crawled in when I wasn't looking."

The doctor lay the purplish baby, all coated with what looked like white grease, on top of Rita's draped belly. "She's ugly and gorgeous at the same time," Louie said. "I mean, she doesn't look like I thought she would."

"She will after I clean her up," the nurse said, waiting for the doctor to give her the go-ahead.

"Care to cut the cord, Dad?"

"Oh, yeah. Thanks, Doc." Louie's face was radiant as he snipped the yellowish banding that had connected mother and baby.

Louie looked back at Rita and his face fell. Her work was done. He knew from their limited time together that she intended to vanish as soon as she could. "Hey," he said, then bent to kiss her on the forehead. "Thank you so much. If there's anything I can ever do for you, I will. I mean, I'd even give you a kidney or half my liver. I'd even give you all my money but I don't have much."

"Just take good care of her," Rita said, sniffing back tears.

"Oh, yeah. No worries about that. And I'll send you lots of pictures, too. Hey, I have to get your email address. I don't even know your last name." He bent and whispered. "Did you give them your real name when you checked in?"

She shook her head minimally, then turned to watch the nurse check the baby over, wiping off the white waxy coating. The nurse put a pink knit cap on the baby's head, swaddled her in a receiving blanket, then brought her over. "You should nurse her right away. It's good for her digestive system but also helps shrink your uterus and stop bleeding."

Rita frowned and turned her head away, overwhelmed.

"Hey," Louie said, gently pulling her face towards him. He made eye contact and said, "This is for you *and* for her. You need to heal. She can help you with that. And you need to help her, too. The nurse said her gut or tummy or something in there can only be fixed by what you can give her. No synthetic drugs for our little girl."

"Not *our*…"

"Okay, would you help *my* little girl. And you need to think about taking good care of yourself, too. Starting right now."

The nurse had been following the conversation and was ready as soon as Rita looked like she was going to assent. She untied her gown, baring her breast.

"Ouch!"

"Yup, for being so little, babies sure have a powerful sucker," the nurse said.

"Yeah, there's that but I swear I can feel my womb shrinking by the suckle."

"It is. We have drugs that are similar, but there's nothing like a baby to get the job done."

"Hey," Louie said. "Can someone take a picture of us?"

"Sure," the nurse said, accepting the phone. "Okay everyone, get in close."

"But I'm nursing," Rita said.

"First home-cooked meal," Louie said. "Now smile."

Rita couldn't help but grin at the silly man. Suddenly, her mood swung to depression and she started to cry.

"Don't worry," the nurse said. "That's going to happen a lot for the next month or so. Sometimes longer. Your hormones are going to be all over the place: happy, sad, angry. The best thing to do is to eat right, drink lots of water, and get plenty of sleep. Of course, taking care of a baby is going to make that part tough, but you're young and can handle it, I'm sure."

Rita's half-hearted smile worked. Louie knew the truth, but the two of them had agreed not to say anything about the baby-sharing arrangements. "Don't you think you ought to let Charlene and the boys know you're a daddy?" she asked.

"Oh, yeah. I'm a daddy. You stay there and don't go anywhere. Hey, nurse lady. Sorry, I forgot your name. Can I bring my nephews in here? They're six but really well-behaved."

"It's up to you two, but I don't think anyone but Mom and Dad should be holding your daughter for a while. She doesn't have any immunity other than what she's getting from Mom right now."

Louie looked over and watched Rita study the baby's face as she nursed. A tingle went from head to toe and up to his groin. His accidental family. They couldn't have been more perfect if he had tried. Even if one portion of it was going to disappear.

***

By the time Louie was back in the room, the baby was back in the layette, sleeping.

"Ew, she's ugly," Chip said.

Carlos nudged him. "You obviously haven't seen newborn puppies. All babies look like that, all wrinkly and stuff, but then in a couple weeks, they're bouncing all over the place and cute."

"It'll be more than a couple of weeks, but yes, she's going to fill out and look like you think babies should soon. Your little sister's going to look pretty much the same," Charlene said. "But I think she's beautiful."

Charlene walked up to Rita and lay her hand on her shoulder, letting Louie ride herd on the boys. "How are you doing?"

"As good as can be expected," she said. "The nurse had me nurse her." She paused. "That sounds funny but it's true. She said it would help shrink my uterus back to normal faster. Hurt like the dickens and so did her suckling. I guess I don't have to get used to that, though. Do you think you'll be able to handle two that way, I mean the nursing?"

"If not, I can always supplement with formula. I'll try, though. That is unless you change your mind."

Rita studied Charlene's face. "You're not backing out on me, are you?" she whispered.

"No. But what about you? After you've nursed her, you're still willing to give her to me?"

"No."

Charlene's eyes widened in shock, then she watched Rita giggle. "I'm not giving her to you. Sorry. That sounded wrong. I'm giving her to her father. You and Louie can make whatever arrangements you want. I know what we said in front of the doctor, but I also know what you and Louie and I said. First order of ownership no matter what, though, is to the daddy. I'm going to be out of here and back to my old life as soon as they'll let me."

"Oh, no you don't. Or please don't. You have to stick around and take care of her when I go into labor. Promise me you'll stay until I'm on my feet."

"Louie can…"

"Can what? He can barely tie his own shoes."

"Hey! I like slip-on boots and shoes." Louie straightened up and added, "It's a personal preference, not a disability"

"And what about your husband? Where's Arlie?"

"Oh, he'll be here." Charlene's face fell, then brightened with false hope. "Because he said so."

"Hey, Uncle Louie. What's her name?" Carlos asked.

"Yeah, huh. What's her name?" Chip giggled into his hands. "Pinkie?"

"Well, we were talking about it earlier," Louie said. "And we decided on Louella."

"He decided on Louella," Rita said.

"No, we decided on Louella. See," he said to the boys as he gently touched the baby's pink hat, "My name is Louis and Rita's middle name is Ella, so together the name is Louella."

"Your name is Rita Ella?" Carlos asked.

Rita frowned. "Sorta. Rita is my nickname. Ella really is my middle name, though. I think Louella will work. She even has enough room for a middle name if he wants."

Chapter 9: Sleeping Beauty

A refrigerated container or reefer is an intermodal container (shipping container) used in intermodal freight transport that is refrigerated for the transportation of temperature-sensitive cargo. https://en.wikipedia.org/wiki/Refrigerated_container

December 23 mid-afternoon

"Hey, Cappy. This is Charlene. Has Arlie checked in? No, he hasn't taken his family leave yet. At least if he did, he didn't tell me. I haven't seen him in two days. I know he was working a case with Louie but believe it or not, Louie's a daddy. Yeah, I know he was just a citizen ride-along but he considered his time with Arlie an internship. He was a little frustrated that there was no one to call when he needed to take the time off, so I told him I'd take care of it. Yup, you heard me right. One hundred percent Louie's little girl. He named her Louella. Yeah, I'll be helping him out with her. No, his relationship with the mother and where they're going in life is his to share or keep to himself. No spoilers from me. Except little Louella is a doll. Red hair and bright blue eyes. She's pretty mellow. Well, I'm concerned about Arlie, so if he calls in, ask him if he's contacted me yet. All right. Merry Christmas to you and yours, too."

Carlos waited until his mother was off the phone, literally putting his hand on Chip's mouth to keep him from interrupting. "Hey, Mom," he asked when she hung up.

"Is Dad gonna be able to play Santa for the Senior Center Christmas party?" Chip asked. "He never told us."

"Hey, I was gonna ask," Carlos said.

Charlene rolled her eyes. "I don't know. Dad's working somewhere that I can't call him, so either Louie will have to or they'll find someone else." She looked at the boys and saw their frowns. "You know he would if he could, right? He's a cop and sometimes that means sacrifices. Which would you rather have him do: play Santa or save someone's life?"

The boys looked at each other but remained mum. Carlos nudged Chip. "I'm thinking, I'm thinking," Chip said. "Okay, if it was someone I knew, yeah, I guess I'd want him to save his life."

"Everyone knows someone, so that means even if you don't know who he's saving, it's someone special, okay? Now, stop being so glum. My back's hurting. Would one of you get me the icepack out of the freezer? I want to put my feet up before I have to fix dinner."

"Here you go," Rita said, handing Charlene the icepack wrapped in a dishtowel. "And don't worry about dinner. I have something started. You know, this is all right. I didn't think Louie would take to being a daddy so quickly. He's doing everything."

"Pbbt," Charlene blew a raspberry as she sat down in her rocker recliner. She put her feet up on the stool and adjusted the icepack. "He's a natural when it comes to nurturing. He had enough uncle experience under his belt before Louella came around that it was a quick transition. He was an uncle for less than a year, too. That guy has a heart the size of a gray whale..."

Charlene stopped talking and her face suddenly paled.

"Are you all right?" Rita asked. "You look like you just swallowed a mouthful of blubber."

"No. I mean," Charlene pulled herself forward, her hands gripping the arms of the chair. "I just felt a ping, like something let loose. Is that what it feels like when your water breaks?"

"Um. No. That's not good." Rita stood in front of Charlene and offered her a hand. "Stand up and let me see."

Charlene stood up and turned around. Both women looked in horror at the bloody spot on the seat. "Crap," Charlene said.

"Couch. Now. Feet up," Rita ordered. She picked up the house phone and dialed 911. "We have a medical emergency. Send an ambulance stat. And if there's someone around with obstetric skills, make sure she's on board. Yeah, well, you get the ambulance coming. I'm hanging up and calling her doctor. No! Bullshit! Okay, then you can stay on the line and I'm calling the OB from my cellphone."

Rita handed the phone to Charlene. "They have some questions for you. Whatever you do, don't freak out. We got this. Between Louie and me and the professionals, you're in good hands. The worst thing you can do is panic. Promise me you won't panic."

Charlene's eyes widened, panic trying to invade.

"Oh, wait," Rita said. "I'll put the ice pack on your back. That should slow the blood flow. I think your placenta broke loose. Feet up, remember? Calm spot. Pretend you're Sleeping Beauty. Take a break from reality. When you wake up, Prince Charming and Baby Charming will be waiting for you. Rest. Peace…"

Rita took the phone from Charlene's stunned hand. "She can't talk right now. Bye," and hung up.

"Peace…" Charlene said, then took slow, deep breaths, sending herself to a Neverland where pain and chaos weren't welcome, where flowers and happiness filled the land.

"What's wrong with Mom?" Chip asked.

"Is she going to be all right?" Carlos echoed in the same frightened tone.

"Let's hope so," Rita said. "She's playing Sleeping Beauty. Go get

Uncle Louie."

"Hey, what's going on?" Louie asked, Louella held to his shoulder.

"Trouble in paradise," she said. "I called the ambulance. You need to stay here with the kids and try to find Arlie. We're going to the hospital."

"Are you sure…" Louie started to ask.

"I'm sure you're better with the boys and LuLu than I am. And I'm pretty sure I'm a little more familiar with female anatomy than you are. Char's preregistered at the hospital, so they have all her info. Crap. I gotta call the OB. I hear the siren now."

Rita bent down close to Charlene's face. "I don't know if you can hear me, but you're doing great with the relaxing, Lady C. It's all under control. All you have to do is stay breathing. I'm serious. All you have to do is breathe. We'll take care of the rest."

Charlene felt the chaos swarm around her: the jostling of her body as the medics lifted her onto the gurney, the clunk-clatter-clatter as it rolled into the ambulance, the little bumps as the rig rolled down the driveway and onto the highway. She could feel the weight of the blankets on top of her, but their initial warmth had left and she was cold. Her body shivered involuntarily but she knew it wasn't the chill of the air but the loss of blood. 'Just keep breathing,' she thought.

She pulled in a shallow breath, held it, then blew it out. *Just breathe.*

***

"Hey, Abby. Do you still have that tracker thingy on Arlie?" Louie asked. "You do? Cool. Can you see where he is? Okay. I'll wait. Hey! Did you hear I'm a daddy now. No, not puppies. I have a real baby. I mean, I have a daughter. Yeah, she was born two days ago. Seven pounds eleven ounces and twenty inches long. Her name's Louella, but I think her nickname's gonna be LuLu. It fits her better. Oh, you can see Charlene, too? I didn't know that. Yeah. She's in rough shape. That's why I'm trying to find Arlie. They just took her to the hospital. Rita — that's my daughter LuLu's birth mother — went with her. She said something about the placebo or something. Oh, yeah. The placenta. So, you can see that Arlie's okay? He's not! What? Where in the deuce is he? Hell, yeah get someone out after him! What? He's halfway to Seattle? How? Okay, I'll get off the phone so you can do your thing. And keep me posted on Charlene, too."

Louie hung up the phone. "Damn!"

"You're not supposed to say that, Uncle Louie."

"Yeah, huh," Chip said.

"Sorry, guys. Sorry, LuLu. Looks like it's just us here tonight. I'm

111

glad Rita got dinner started."

"Hey! I got an idea," Carlos said. "We were supposed to go to the Senior Center dinner tonight. Why don't you just turn off the crockpot and we can all go? You can stuff the baby in that wrap thing and put the Santa costume on top of it. You won't even need padding."

"I don't have a costume," Louie said.

"It's at the Senior Center," Carlos said with exaggerated patience, "So it doesn't get lost."

"Yeah, 'cause the real Santa already has his," Chip said. "This is just for the pretend Santa. That can be you tonight. Come on, Louie. It's gonna be boring if we stay here. Besides, you and Rita promised us that Mom's just playing Sleeping Beauty at the hospital 'til they can take the baby out. We can go see them tomorrow."

"Yeah, 'cause what are we gonna do if we stay home? Watch the crockpot boil?" Carlos asked.

"All right, everyone," Louie agreed. "Off we go into the great gray north of the Chugiak-Eagle River Senior Center." He picked up the keys on the counter and remote started the minivan. "Go potty, guys while I pack a fresh bottle for LuLu."

***

Carlos ran ahead and pressed the giant buttons for the automatic doors at the center. "Hey! They started without us! And Santa's already here."

"Yeah, the pretend Santa," Chip whispered.

Louie followed behind them, the infant car seat draped with a receiving blanket to keep out the chill. "Remember your manners," he called out after them.

Chip found an empty table and set down his die-cast cars, then ran to his brother. "Hey, I found our names on the table," he said, then looked up to see why Carlos was so quiet. "Grandpa?" he asked.

"Ho, ho, ho," the big man said, his pillow-stuffed outfit still two sizes too big.

Carlos whispered to Chip, "Yeah, I think it's Grandpa, but let's pretend so the seniors don't know. They think he's the real guy."

Louie followed with car seat in hand, the dozing baby snug in her blanket-filled carrier. "Hey, I know that guy!"

"Of course, you do," the Judge said, a quick scowl of admonishment popping in, then melting into a smile at seeing his family. "I'm Santa Claus!"

"But Louie and LuLu were going to play Santa," Carlos said.

"Who's LuLu?"

Louie lifted the carrier and saluted the Judge with her. "Oh, yeah. Glad to see you again, Santa. Congratulations! It's a girl. Another girl. The other one will be here soon. I hope."

"Another girl?" he asked.

"Yeah. Here's another one for your Nice Kids' list. This is my daughter, LuLu. Her real name is Louella but we call her LuLu. When you get a chance, I need to talk to you. In private."

"Ho, ho, ho," the Judge said, his eyes narrowed in concern but voice boisterous. "Maybe these two fine young men will help me hand out gifts to the residents. Boys, do you think you can be Santa's elves tonight?"

"Yeah! Yeah! Grandpa. I mean, Santa," Chip said.

"Yeah, we know everyone here, just in case you forgot their names," Carlos said, then giggled into his hand.

The young woman named Tiffany brought over a laundry basket filled with wrapped presents. "Here you go, Santa."

The Judge reached in the basket. "This one says Tony. Can you two help me find Tony?"

The boys both pointed to the older man in the wheelchair, hunched over, inspecting something on the table.

"It's not polite to point, men," Santa said, frowning, then bringing back the feigned smile. *Something is wrong here. Where's my*

114

daughter? Why didn't he say something? Crap! That's why he wants to talk to me in private!

"Yes, sir," both boys said, quickly tucking their pointing fingers under their armpits, holding onto Santa with their other hands, leading him to the man inspecting the coin on the table in front of him.

"Ho, ho, ho. Merry Christmas, Tony," Santa said, handing him the present. "My helpers here will help you open it if you want. We have to make this quick, though. I have a lot to do before Christmas morning."

Louie watched the Judge and the boys make the rounds, then noticed the Judge's wife in the corner. "Hey, Lara. I didn't see you there. I thought you two were Outside until after the new year."

Lara's eyes widened at seeing the baby carrier. "Did Charlene already have her baby? My, God! We cut the trip short when they moved up her due date. Where is she? Is she okay? Is this her? My granddaughter?" Lara babbled as she pulled aside the covering, looking for the baby swaddled within.

"Um, lots of questions but I'll do my best. Yes, you're her grandma, but no, she's not Charlene and Arlie's baby. This is my daughter, LuLu. Charlene isn't okay, though. She's at the hospital. There wasn't anything we could do, so Rita — that's LuLu's birth mother — told me to stay with the boys. We decided we would come here and help the residents celebrate Christmas rather than watch the crockpot boil. I was going to be Santa and LuLu in her sling was going to be my belly. Imagine my surprise when I found the Judge here."

"Louie. Stop right there. You already have given me more than I can process. Charlene's at the hospital? What happened?"

"It's baby stuff. Complications. We told the boys she's just playing Sleeping Beauty until the baby gets here. Honestly, though, waiting is harder than I thought it'd be. At least, not being in the same building. I'm ready to go play tag team in the hospital waiting room with Rita. I mean, when Rita was having our baby, that's what Charlene and I did."

Lara stood up and grabbed her coat. "We're going now. I'll go make an excuse for Santa."

"Okay, but…" Louie said, then realized she had already made up her mind. He'd been around women long enough to know that once a woman had set her goal, there was no changing her course.

"Hey, Tiffany," Louie said to the director. "Change of plans. The boys and I have to leave. I guess Santa and his wife are coming, too. Oh, and my daughter. This is LuLu. You'll be seeing more of her, I'm sure. Sorry we missed dinner. We were really hungry, too."

"Hold on. I'll be right back. I'll just have Jeff throw everything into giant tortillas and make Christmas wraps for you. Three large and two littles? You can eat them when you get home."

"Sounds like a plan. Oh, wait, can you make it four bigs and two littles? I'm really hungry," Louie said, omitting the fact that they were heading to the hospital, not home. She didn't need to know that. Still, real food sounded good. He'd get one for Rita, too. There had to be an upside somewhere to this messed-up night and it looked like a Christmas Eve eve turkey and stuffing burrito dinner with family at the hospital was it.

Chapter 10: Hospitals, Ambulances, and ERs, oh my!

In the past 15 years the number of hospitals per capita has decreased in both the U.S. and comparably wealthy OECD countries, on average. The density of hospitals in the U.S. has decreased somewhat faster since 1995 (by about 21%, compared to an average decrease of about 3% in comparable countries).
https://www.healthsystemtracker.org/chart-collection/u-s-health-care-resources-compare-countries/#item-start
(The Organization for Economic Cooperation and Development (OECD) is a unique forum where the governments of 34 democracies with market economies work with each other, as well as with more than 70 non-member economies to promote economic growth, prosperity, and sustainable development.)

December 23 evening

"How come we're going back there? Is the hospital where they take all the babies out?" Chip asked.

"They do all sorts of fancy stuff there," Carlos said to his brother. "Plus, it's where the doctors and nurses hang out when they're not at their offices. I don't know if the dentists do, though," Carlos added. "Hey! Where's Grandma and Grandpa?"

"They're coming in their car," Louie said. "Now, I want you on your best behavior 'cause if you don't, we're all going home and just sit around and do laundry or something. No fun stuff, for sure."

"When we're in the waiting room, can we eat our Christmas burritos?" Chip asked.

"Yeah, that's a great idea. They sure do smell good." Louie glanced up in the mirror and verified what he thought he had heard. "It sounds like they're even making LuLu hungry."

"She's too little for burritos," Carlos said.

"Yeah, huh," Chip added. "Because she doesn't have teeth yet. Hey, are we there yet?"

"Pretty soon, guys. Pretty soon." Louie clicked the icon on the dash, then selected a few more options, winding up with voice to text for Rita. "Hey, Rita. The kids and I are on our way. Can you meet us out front in five minutes? Thanks. Louie."

Rita waited in the lobby, then stepped outside when she saw the minivan pull up, stomping her feet and rubbing her upper arms to try to get warm.

"Where's your coat?" Louie asked.

"Didn't bring one. Do you need a hand?"

"Yeah. Can you get LuLu or her diaper bag? I gotta get her a bottle. I got some food for us, too. Guys, bring dinner and your cars or tablets or whatever." Louie handed the keys to the valet, then started to take off his coat and give it to Rita.

"No, thanks. I'll be fine once we're inside."

The boys rushed past the adults and baby, seeking out their old stomping grounds: the waiting room. Carlos used the sleeve of his coat to brush away the pile of magazines on the coffee table. "Stack 'em up or put them somewhere else," Louie said.

"Then go wash your hands," Rita added.

"Man, this is like having *four* parents," Carlos said. "We'll never get a break!"

Louie pawed through the diaper bag, looking for the pre-mixed bottle of formula he had put in before they left the house. "Dang! I know the bottle is in here somewhere. And where can I heat it up? Maybe it's still in the car."

"Give her to me, Dad," Rita said. "I got it covered. Toss me a burp rag, will you?"

"Huh?" Louie looked up and realized she was getting ready to nurse LuLu. "I thought you didn't want to do that bonding thing."

"Just hand me a burb rag or cloth or whatever you want to call it, please!"

"Yeah, sure," he said, handing it to her. He watched as she stuffed it up her shirt and into her bra on the side opposite the hungry baby. "What's that for?"

"I'm discovering all sorts of random facts about my anatomy. When she nurses on one side, the milk lets down on the other side at the same time."

"Lets down?" Louie asked.

"Ooh," she sighed as the baby latched on.

"Are you two okay?" Louie asked.

"Oh, yeah." Rita closed her eyes at that odd combination of pain, relief, and bliss, relaxing into the bliss part. She took a moment for herself then looked at Louie. "I'll tell you what. You and I can have a little New Mother Anatomy 101 class after all this gets settled. In the meantime, I think I really do need her as much as she needs me. I can't imagine running to find bottles and nipples and formula when what she needs is literally hanging off my chest. Whether you want me or not, Louie, I think you're stuck with me for a few weeks."

"Yeah, well, I kinda thought you were nursing her when no one was looking. She didn't really want to take the bottle when I knew it'd been four hours. It's okay if you hang around for a while. I mean, whether it's until Charlene gets back on her feet or twenty years, it's fine with us."

"You really are a wonderful man, Louie," Rita said, reaching out to touch his arm. "I'm pretty much taking this minute by minute. This is definitely part emotional bonding and part physical need. Whether

I had ever nursed her or not, my milk would still have come in. I know it's best for her, and right now, until life gets settled, how about we share the baby care?"

"Sounds good to me. We'll both get more sleep. When you're done there, I want to introduce you to the Judge and his wife. He's Charlene's dad and she's the new wife. The first one died, but this one's pretty cool, too. She already claimed LuLu as her granddaughter earlier at the Senior Center. Last year when Carlos's mother died, the two of them didn't even blink about taking him as their grandson even though he's not Charlene's blood. They kinda claimed me, too."

"What a wonderful family LuLu's getting."

"You, too. I mean, by default you're part of our family, too. Look over there." Louie stood up and moved over to Rita's other side.

Rita looked up and saw the Judge and his wife waving hello to her and Louie. She lifted her free hand and gave a finger flutter, then set her hand back down on the baby. "I don't know what I did to deserve all this, but I'm definitely grateful."

Louie stood up and waved at them, then squatted back down next to her. "Not nearly as grateful as we all are for you."

"You are so sappy. Cute, loveable, and sappy."

"And thanks to you, a daddy."

"Hey, before the boys start asking…" Louie watched as the boys spread paper towels on top of the low coffee table, creating a homey setting for their foil-wrapped burritos. "What's going on with Charlene?"

"They put her in a coma. Or she went into one by herself and they're keeping her there. They're waiting until she stabilizes, and then they want to do a C-section. They can't do anything without her or her husband's authorization, though."

"How about her dad's? He's a judge, so if there's a legal way to do it, he'd know how."

"What about Arlie? Where's he?"

"Abby's looking," Louie said, then realized she didn't know who she was. "Abby's Arlie's work buddy. They have all these cool apps. She put a tracker in Arlie a while back. And I mean *in* him, not on him. She can see what his heart's doing and where he is and all that stuff. I talked to her earlier and she said he was somewhere in the Pacific."

"Pacific Ocean?" Rita asked, then lifted the baby up to burp her.

"Yeah, I trust Abby to send a crew out to fetch him. I guess his vitals showed he was stressed or hurt or something. Sometimes you just have to leave that shit — I mean, stuff — to the professionals."

Lara and the Judge came to see the boys in the waiting room.

"Hey, guys."

Louie waved his hand in the air. "I'll be right there, Judge. I mean, Dad."

Rather than wait, the Judge came to him. "Is this Charlene's daughter? Where is she?"

Lara joined them, noticed the spot where milk had leaked on the front of Rita's shirt, and deduced that this was Louie's daughter's mother. "No, silly. This is our other granddaughter, LuLu, Louie's daughter. She's the one I told you about. Hi, I'm Lara, the grandmother. Or the other grandma, depending on how many there are."

"Rita," she said, intentionally leaving off the fake last name she'd been using for five months. "And yes, you're the only grandmother." Rita placed the baby in Lara's opened arms. "I was just telling Louie what's going on. I'll start from the top. Charlene's in ICU. Short story is they need to perform a C-section to get the baby out but need authorization from her, the father or I hope, the next of kin. That would be you."

"Why can't she give the authorization herself?" the Judge asked.

"She's sorta in a coma. She lost a lot of blood. She could have died, but we moved fast."

Louie saw the Judge's legs start to falter and reached out, grabbing him in an awkward bear hug. "Hold on there, Dad."

The Judge let Louie help him to a chair. "Where's Arlie?"

"Undercover, I guess. Abby's looking for him now," Louie said. He leaned in and whispered, "Oh, and we told the boys that their mom is playing Sleeping Beauty. We're hoping that just like the storybook character, she'll wake up when her Prince Charming shows up and gives her a quick kiss."

"Or a long kiss or even a boot in the pants. How'd this happen?" he asked, fanning his face with an old magazine.

"Placenta previa," Rita said. "It was a miracle that it was only a partial separation. If I hadn't laid her out right away or she had started running around and freaking out, it might have separated completely. As it is, the baby's still getting what she needs. If Charlene starts into labor, though, everything could start shifting or pulling away. That's why she's in ICU and on drugs."

"Okay. That's it." The judge set his magazine down and stood up. "Take me to wherever it is I need to sign those papers. I'm not waiting for Arlie. Not one damned good thing can happen with waiting. That baby's big enough to breathe air now." He looked around and saw no one else was standing. "Well?"

"I can take you back," Louie said. "Looks like Grandma has LuLu, Rita, and the boys under control."

The Judge put his hand on Louie's shoulder. "Lead the way, son. By the way, I think that by giving Lara a granddaughter, you put her into Seventh Heaven a few hours early. Or maybe she'll jump up to Eighth Heaven when the next one gets here."

"Yeah, let's hope so. I was there when LuLu was born. There's no way Charlene can deliver a baby in the shape she's in now, all zonked out and stuff. That's hard work!"

"Yes, it is. Hey. Who's this gal Rita?"

"Oh, she's my daughter's mother."

"I kinda figured that, but I thought you were, you know, gay."

"Well, for at least one night I wasn't. She wasn't either. What we both were, though, is drunk."

"Ah, a tequila child. Lots of them in the world. Still a blessing, no matter how they got started."

Thunk! Scuffle.

"Get away from me, you pig!"

Everyone looked toward the noise. Three officers, one of them plainclothes, were just outside the emergency room entrance, trying to usher in a belligerent female, her hands cuffed behind her back, her black leather jacket bloodstained and ripped.

"Do you have her?" Rita asked, her face pale and unemotional as she nodded to Grandma.

126

"What? Sure," Lara said, LuLu bundled up and held close.

Rita walked outside to get a closer look and verify what she already knew. She stepped up to the resisting and restraining foursome and remained a cautious ten feet away. The bigger city cop glanced at her, then looked away, not sensing a threat. "I thought you were supposed to leave the trash in the dumpster," Rita said caustically.

"You bitch!" the prisoner screamed. "I thought that was you I saw at the restaurant."

Rita grinned, reveling in the fact that she was free and unencumbered. Her former beauty-queen gorgeous girlfriend Kitty was not only injured, her hair was askew, the hairpiece barely hanging on by a few strands. Bloodshot eyes ringed with thick black circles of sweat and tear-streaked makeup glared at Rita. The three large official-looking men grunted as they worked to physically restrain her. It didn't take a genius to see they were taking her to jail after whatever wound she had was treated.

"Meow," Rita said, then laughed.

"Argh!" Kitty lunged at Rita, briefly escaping one officer's hold. She made it to within two feet of Rita when the plainclothesman grabbed her hair. Unfortunately, what he caught was the lingering hairpiece. Rita saw her opportunity and took it.

Fwap!

Kitty was felled by the unexpected blow, the swift left-handed punch stunning her, sending her stumbling backward into the plainclothes cop. Blood spurted from her mouth and nose. She turned her head sideways and spat out the tooth. "Shit!"

"Oops," Rita said and turned away.

"What the?" the larger cop asked, then shook his head and picked up Kitty by the cuffs, pulling her to her feet and dragging her towards the admitting desk.

"What was that all about?" the Judge asked Louie, then he changed his mind, shaking his head. "No, don't tell me. It's on a need to know basis."

"Old girlfriend," Louie whispered. "I'm sure she deserved it."

The driver of the undercover cop car came running out. "Hey! Rita! What are you doing here?"

"Jesse? Wow! What a beard you have there. Um, I'm staying out of trouble. Sort of. And you?"

"Just finishing up a deep undercover project. I don't know if you know it or not, but that skank you just punched out was busted with five keys of meth and a container full of kids destined for The Corridor."

"Who? What? You're an undercover cop? And what in the hell is

The Corridor?"

"Shush. The cop thing is a secret. I'm FBI but we joint venture with other agencies every once in a while. The I-5 Corridor. Lots of human trafficking going on there. You wouldn't know it to see it. All those missing kids, the runaways that you try to bring in off the streets?"

"Yeah…"

"Well, you're not just saving them from prostitution. It gets worse. Not just sex slaves, but if they're the right profile, they harvest their organs. The lucky ones get to move on with just one kidney. The others…" He shook his head.

"Jesse, I think I'm gonna be sick."

"Let me go park the car and I'll be right in. You are okay, aren't you? I never expected you to leave the kids in the Seattle area."

"Long story. Catch you in a few."

Rita walked through the entrance toward the waiting room. Suddenly, she wanted to hug her baby and the boys more than anything in the world. She needed to hold onto a healthy, secure, and loved person who was out of harm's way.

"Are you going to be okay?" Lara asked.

"Did the boys see what I did?"

"No, they were under the table, playing parking garage or some nonsense. Here, hold Lulu. She'll make you feel better."

Tears poured down Rita's cheeks as she cuddled her little bundle of cotton flannel and flesh. The little squirms on the outside were a delight, so familiar to the ones she had felt when pregnant. "You grow up to be a good person," she said through her tears. "And no hanging around mean people. Mean people suck."

Lara put her arm around Rita's shoulders. "You said I'm the only grandmother. Does that mean your mother is dead?"

Rita shrugged but didn't say a word, just continued to hold her daughter and sway in place, secure in Lara's arms as the two moved together.

"Well, you definitely have one now. I never birthed a child, but now I have Charlene and Louie and you. Oh, and Arlie when he gets back. I hope he's okay. I don't have that icky feeling, so I'm sure he is."

"Where's Louie?"

"He and the Judge went back to make things right. Pretty sure, I'll have another granddaughter real soon. Let's hope all goes well on that end, too."

"What's going on here?" Louie asked, looking around. "And the boys?"

"We're down here, running over zombies with our cars in the

basement parking garage."

"Good plan. Stay put, would ya?"

"No worries. We don't want to get our brains eaten," Carlos said.

"Yeah, we might need 'em sometime," Chip added, then went back to *vrooming.*

The Judge came up and put his arms around his wife, Rita, and baby LuLu. "They're taking her back right away. We'll have another little girl in the family in less than half an hour."

"And Charlene will be okay, right?" Louie asked.

"Should be. As soon as they have all her insides fixed up, they'll take her off that coma drip and she'll come out of it naturally. Any word on Arlie yet?"

Louie pulled out his phone and looked for texts. "Nope. Not yet."

"Hey, Rita," a voice called out. "I don't mean to interrupt, but I'm on a tight schedule here. Can you spare me a minute?"

All eyes turned to the handsome man with the thickest, blackest beard ever seen on a white man. "Jess?" Louie asked softly.

Rita looked at Louie. "You know him?" she said, then went limp in the knees. "Jess. Jesse. Oh, crap. He's your Jesse, huh?"

"Well, he was. What? Was he your boyfriend, too?"

"Hello? I'm right here. I can hear what you're saying. Hey, Louie. Long time, no see. Sorry I couldn't call. I figured you'd understand

131

working undercover, you being a friend of Arlie's and all."

"You said you were FBI. I didn't know you ever went undercover. I thought it was your way of dumping me. And is she your girlfriend?" Louie put his arm around Rita's shoulder, pulling her and his daughter close.

Rita squirmed at the unfamiliar show of affection but didn't try to pull away. "No, he's not my boyfriend," she said. "We worked together in Seattle. Sort of. He was doing stuff off the radar. I was giving him information. Oh, shit! That's why Kitty left! She found out where my safe houses were! That's what happened!"

"It's okay," Jesse said. "We had a mole who let us know that she — or whoever it was — was shopping around for street-experienced girls. We moved them into an aftercare facility before she found them. You totally dropped off everyone's radar so we couldn't let you know. Hey, what did happen to you?"

Rita held up the baby and grinned sheepishly.

Jesse's eyes widened and jaw dropped.

"Yeah, and she's mine. I mean, the baby. She's ours. Mine and Rita's. And we're still working things out but no matter what, I'm her daddy forever and ever. And if you don't like it, you can just come get the key to our shared storage locker and clear out your stuff."

Jesse looked from Rita to Louie and then back again. "Well, that explains a lot. I didn't think anything on heaven or earth would ever bust you away from taking care of the street kids." He pulled the covering down from the baby's face. "I guess a little bit of heaven *and* earth could pull you away, though. She's beautiful. What's her name?"

"Louella," Rita said.

"Yeah, Lou after me and Ella after her mother. But we call her LuLu."

"Hey, little LuLu. You be good to your mommy and daddy, all right." Jesse looked at Rita. "You know, I was going to talk to you, and I will later, but I think I have some major apologizing to do to Louie. I don't know if you know it, but he and I kinda had a thing going on before I, ahem, had to leave in a hurry."

"So, you're the one who caught Kitty?" she asked.

"No, actually it was an Alaskan cop. Arlie Biggar, Louie's friend. He's in back right now getting his shoulder fixed up. He and one of his ride-alongs were shot. Kitty threw them into a reefer trailer with a bunch of young girls and guys from the Bush. The feds intercepted the steamer on the way to Tacoma. It's a good thing, too. The temperature got pretty low, even with their shared body heat in an insulated trailer."

"Hey! I gotta jet. If Arlie's in back, he might not know his wife is here. She's having their baby. Or rather, they're taking it out of her while she's zonked out."

"Oh, no. Shoot. He was delirious, or at least we thought he was. His phone was shot. Literally shot, but it saved his life. It deflected the bullet up so he was only zapped in the shoulder. Still, he was in rough surroundings, without water and only broccoli to eat. His boss knows what's going on, though. A gal named Abby?"

"Abby's not technically the boss. Cap is, but Abby knows about as much as anyone else." Louie bent down and kissed Rita on the top of the head. "Be back in a sec, hon."

As soon as Louie was out of earshot, Jesse bent down. "Are you trying to take my guy?"

"You'd better be good to him," Rita said. "No, he's not my guy, but we do share a daughter. Next time you go anywhere, even for a cup of coffee, you tell him where and how long 'til you get back, all right?"

"Each and every time," he said.

Chapter 11: The Beauty Awakens

About 60% of the glucose and oxygen use by the brain is meant for its electrical activity and the rest for all other activities such as metabolism. When barbiturates are given to brain-injured patients for induced coma, they act by reducing the electrical activity of the brain, which reduces the metabolic and oxygen demand. https://en.wikipedia.org/wiki/Induced_coma

Recovery room
Christmas Eve morning

"Hey, there, Sleeping Beauty. It's time to wake up and see your little princess."

Arlie looked up at the nurse. "Can you see a difference in her stats or whatever? Do you think she heard me?"

The nurse shook her head. "Nope. Nada. I think you'll just have to give her a little time for the barbituates to flush out of her system. We want it to be gradual, so maybe this is a good thing."

"Do you think maybe seeing the baby will make a difference?"

"Hey," Louie said, sticking his head into the room. "Is it okay if I come in and see how my sister's doing?"

The nurse looked at Arlie, her eyes asking the silent question. It was his decision.

"Yeah, come on in, Louie. How's everyone doing?"

"As well as can be expected, I suppose. Hey, I want to make a suggestion. I mean, it sounds kinda dumb coming from me, but I am an experienced dad now and all. After Rita delivered, they had her nurse LuLu right away. I know Charlene had a cesarean and all, but do you think that would work?" Louie asked, looking at the nurse.

"It won't hurt her. It's up to Dad."

"I'm willing to try anything." Arlie reached over and fumbled with the ties on her gown. "What am I supposed to do here?"

"You'd better let the nurse help you," Louie said. "I know what to do, but I don't want to see Charlene's boob or nothin'."

"Allow me," the nurse said. She pushed the rocker switch and brought the head of the bed up higher. "Hold onto her shoulders so she doesn't slump forward or to either side."

"Thanks," Arlie said, taking the baby from Louie. "Now what?"

"Just rub the nipple on the baby's cheek," the nurse said. "She'll find it." The baby's face quickly turned to find the source of dinner and latched on. "Great reflexes."

Charlene moaned but didn't awaken. After a minute, the baby's mouth dropped away. Asleep. "She's tired from being born, even if it was a C-section. Let me put her back in the bassinette. We'll try again when she wakes up. I'll put a note in her chart that we want to try this before giving her a bottle. At least for the first day."

"First day?" Arlie squeaked. "How long will my wife be out?"

"Like the doctor said, there's no way of telling. Sometimes once the body gets into that comatose state, it wants to stay there. I'll be back in a minute. Push the call button if you need anything."

"I'm sorry, Arlie," Louie said. "And here we thought that Charlene was going to be taking care of two babies and Rita was going to split. Dang! There's gotta be something we can do!"

"How's my little girl?" the Judge said, looking into the room.

"She's still out," Arlie answered, sniffing back the tears. "Why wasn't I here for her?"

"Stop beating yourself up. It would have wound up the same way, whether you were in Chugiak or in Cambodia. Her body had a glitch. She and the baby are both alive. She just needs time, all right?"

"That's easy enough to say, but the guilt is crushing me."

"I'm sorry, I'm sorry," Lara said. "They slipped away."

"Hey, Mom!" Carlos said. "Wake up! Tomorrow's Christmas! We get to open a present tonight, remember? You told us we could."

"Hey," Chip said, walking to the other side of her bed to stand next to his dad. "She isn't playing right. Dad, kiss her again. You're her Prince Charming. You're supposed to wake her up with a kiss.

You must not have done it right."

Arlie wiped his nose with the back of his sleeve then bent close. "Honey, it's time to wake up. Our sons are here and they say it's time. Game's over." He kissed her gently on the forehead.

"Not there," Carlos said. "It's gotta be on the lips."

"Yeah, huh," Chip said. "Kiss her on the lips for a long time like in the movies."

Arlie did as directed but still nothing.

"Okay. We got this, Dad," Carlos said. "Time for Plan B. Come here, Chip."

Chip went to the other side of the bed and held his brother's hand. "Wake up!" they screamed in unison.

The Judge covered his ears, the baby woke up and started squalling, and Arlie and Louie said, "Hush!" all at the same time, but it was Charlene who everyone paid attention to.

"Don't yell in the house, boys," she groused, then turned her head to the side and saw Arlie. "You're here," she whispered and smiled.

"You did it, guys! You woke up your mother!" he said, fresh tears streaming.

"Hey, what's going on?" Charlene reached down to rub her belly as she always did when she woke up. "What? Where's my baby?" she screeched, her arms flailing, cords and tubing catching on pillows and call buttons as she lost it. "What happened? Where am I"

"Whoa! Whoa! Whoa!" Arlie said, his hands fumbling as he tried to find a gentle way to get her to calm down and lie back into the pillows. "Our little girl's asleep in the bassinette. Or was. Louie, would you get Baby Biggar for her mother?"

"Sure thing. Here you are, Charlene. All seven and a half pounds of her. She was a little smaller than LuLu but not much. I didn't watch this one come out, but I gotta tell you, it had to be a lot easier than when Rita had our baby."

As soon as she saw her, Charlene calmed down. "Oh, she's beautiful! And she has red hair, too."

The nurse had watched the ado from outside the room, the boys wake-up call having caught her attention, too. "Everything all right in here?"

"Yes, ma'am. Very all right."

***

"Are you sure you're ready to go home?" Arlie asked. "I mean, the doctor said you can stay here another day or two if you'd like?"

"No, sir! You're taking me home and starting your two months of family leave right now. No excuses. This world can turn without you pushing and shoving it, Arlie Biggar."

"Okay, but a few folks wanted to come say hi. I figured it was better for them to see you here where the nurses can kick them out if they overstay their welcome than at our place where it's too easy for them to get comfortable and hang out."

Charlene reached up and grabbed the big metal ring suspended by a chain above her head and pulled herself upright. "I will miss this, though. At least, until I get my abdominal muscles back."

"Don't worry. We got that covered. We rented a hospital bed complete with all the trapeze tools a recovering woman could want."

"You know what we don't have, though?" she asked, her eyes narrowed which meant he was in trouble.

Arlie lifted his arms and patted himself down, making a joke out of checking for missing body parts.

"A name for our daughter."

"Oh, yeah. I know we were talking about that for what, the last six or eight months."

"Yes," she said, "And we're no closer today than when we found out we were pregnant. I know Louie wanted the name Louise, but now that he has his own daughter, LuLu and Louise might be a little confusing."

Knock. Knock.

"Oh, hey, Li'l Boy. We were just talking about you. Sort of.

Honey," he said, turning to Charlene, "This is the guy who saved my life."

"Hey, you're giving me too much credit, Arlie. I only provided a chunk of the dumb luck. I think that fancy titanium case on your phone helped a lot."

"Well, that and your gun, but I was just getting ready to tell her about our conversation in the reefer unit."

"Which one? Where you, me, and the hijacked kids solved the world's problems or where they gave you yet another version of 'Charles' to name your daughter."

"The latter. Charlene," Arlie said, holding her hand in his. "I'd be honored, flattered, whatever you want to call it, if you'd consider the name Harlie."

"Well, yes, I'd consider it, but don't you think hollering Arlie and Harlie might sound the same?"

"Actually, I thought of that. I want to add a middle name." Arlie looked at his big friend who was frowning in confusion. "Li'l Boy, I know I didn't talk to you about this, but I looked up your real name. I'd like to name our little girl Harlie Jae. Kind of like your first name Jay, but spelled J-A-E."

Arlie looked deep into Charlene's eyes, searching for her gut answer before she issued one of her, 'We'll see,' responses that meant it was a no-go.

"Harlie Jae, quit pulling your brother's hair. Harlie Jae, get down from there! Yeah, I like that." She smiled and nodded. "Yeah, that definitely works."

"Hey Jae, wanna go skating? How about some ice cream, Hey Jae?" Li'l Boy said. "I like that, too. I'd be honored to have your kid named after me, even if it is a middle name for a girl."

"Girls are cool," Charlene said, her lips pursed, ready to defend her gender.

"Oh, yeah, for sure," Li'l Boy said. "I have a daughter, and her mother's about as tough as they come. She was second-string tackle in high school until she messed up her shoulder."

"And they're even getting into the professional sports that normally only have guys," Arlie said. "Remember hearing about that gal in the minors, one of the fastest pitchers ever? Loren Forrest of the Tempe Tornadoes. Now she's one to watch."

"Yeah, well, watch out for our girls when they grow up," Charlene said. "Whether they wind up as doctors, lawyers, judges, or tennis racket re-stringers, they'll be the best ever."

"They?" Arlie asked. "Did I miss something?"

"Yeah, well, about that. You, me, and Louie need to talk..." Charlene shifted in the bed. "LuLu's going to be hanging out with us for a while. A long while."

"And her daddy, too," Louie popped in.

Arlie shrugged a shoulder. "The more, the merrier. And you know why?"

"Why?" Charlene asked.

"Because you said so."

"Yup. And sometimes that's all it takes."

The End

Afterword

Thank you so much for reading ***Because You Said So***, part of ***Sweet and Sassy Holiday***

If it feels like there's more to this story, there is. This is the fifth in the Arlie Undercover series. Find out how Arlie met Charlie and the boys and how Louie came into his life in the first books.

Part One is ***A Stingray Christmas***

Part Two is ***The Biggest Heart Ever***

Part Three is ***Always a Bigger Fish***

Part Four is ***How to Fix a Broken Life***

Follow me at Dani Haviland Street Team to get the latest release dates and early previews of covers and stories.

http://bit.ly/2DaniStTeam

Oh, and pretty please… Would you take a moment to leave a review for this story and/or the box set on Amazon or Goodreads? Your insights help other readers decide if a book is a good fit for them. It's also the invigorating serum that gives authors the feedback they thrive on. Thanks!

Other Books by Dani Haviland

ARLIE UNDERCOVER SERIES

(romantic suspense based in Alaska and Arizona)

A Stingray Christmas: (First book) Anchorage detective on medical leave travels from Alaska to Arizona to see for the first time the son he'd fathered as an anonymous sperm donor. Great and rotten surprises await the cop with the smartest smartphone around.

The Biggest Heart Ever: (Book two) When would Arlie learn that trying to do everything by himself could be deadly—and make Charlene a widow before they were married?

Always a Bigger Fish: (Book three) Back in Alaska, Arlie finds out he's a target. Will vacationing detective Billy Burke (from THE FAIRIES SAGA) have information to help nab the scalper?

How to Fix a Broken Life: (Book four) When Arlie's very pregnant wife is kidnapped by pseudo terrorists, will he be the one to rescue her or will a surprise hero come in to save the day?

Because You Said So: (Book Five) Can Arlie handle two very pregnant women, a terrorist at the Port, and still have time to wear the Santa suit?

THE FAIRIES SAGA SERIES

(historical fiction/time travel, listed in order with novellas):

Kibbles and Bits: FREE ebook! Sample the first stories in the series before you buy. The Fairies Saga stories. Find out how the first five books got their crazy names, too.

Naked in the Winter Wind: FREE ebook! (lengthy novel) How does an older woman wind up as a young hottie in Revolutionary War era North Carolina? First book in the time travel series.

Ha'Penny Jenny: (historical novella) More about the naïve and psychic young girl who was adopted into a time traveling family. Will her past catch up to her?

Aye, I am a Fairy: (lengthy novel) Young British lord finds himself entwined with a time traveling family and must decide if he should go back in time, too. Second book in the series.

Dances Naked: (novel) Directionally challenged time traveler is rescued by Cherokee in 18th century. What must he do before the chief will show him to The Trees, the portal through time?

Chasing Christmas: (historical novella) A young Cherokee is rescued from an abusive man and changes the lives of many in this 18th century America family.

The Great Big Fairy: (lengthy novel) Very tall Benji grew up in the 20th century but was born in the 18th. When he finds a way to return to his grandparents in the distant past, he goes for it. Once there, he realizes he can't stay, but must return to the future. Fourth book in the series.

Little Bear and the Ladies: (historical novella) What's a bachelor trapper to do with all the females he rescues from the Hessian mercenaries? He'd better hurry and figure something!

Little Drummer Boy: (historical novella) Young Scout works to earn money for a home in post-Revolutionary War America but runs up against prejudices and snowstorms.

Never Too Young: (historical novella) Scout and Ha'Penny Jenny have grown up, but will they be able to spend their life together, or will the past and ruffians get in their way?

Time in a Little Blue Bottle: (time travel 'mash up' novella) Elvis, Mark Twain, and the prime vampire are racing to get the bottle of Fountain of Youth water before sweet Bella and the youthful pickpocket. So why are time travelers Marty Melbourne and Master Simon interested?

CONTEMPORARY NOVELLAS – BENJI, THE LOST YEARS

Luke the Unexpected: Love of classic motorcycles brought them together, but Luke and Holly have other challenges to face. Find out how their friend Benji got his stripes here.

Pool Boy Wanted: No Experience Preferred: (rather racy) Young Benji has been a hostage and slave, but life gets worse when an older woman decides she wants him as her own.

STAND ALONE NOVELLAS

(contemporary romances)

Kit Kringle: An Alaskan Tale: Kay moved to Alaska for the wrong reasons, then decided to stay and start her own business. What she hadn't planned on were prejudices and falling in love.

Be My Angel: Wyatt's dream to help save the wild mustangs began with the purchase of a rundown ranch in western Oregon. What he hadn't anticipated was being mesmerized by a sassy woman in a wheelchair.

Three Are One: The post chaplain tried to help the young widow adjust, but would his feelings for her and the search for his lost sister cause problems?

One Arctic Summer: That unforgettable summer of 1994 in Barrow, Alaska, and the touch she never forgot…If she goes back, will he remember her?

The Polar Xpress: Will the California chiropractor get a first chance at romance with the owner of Second Chance Kennels when he is stranded in Alaska?

Too Fast For You: Ten years after Little League, two talented professional baseball players wind up on the same minor league team. Will she remember him? And will their friendship be ruined if she does?

About the Author

 USA Today bestselling author and entrepreneur Dani Haviland started writing late in life and has been making up for lost time with a torrential flood of romances. Tackling everything from historicals to suspense to paranormal themes—and sometimes smashing them together—she even tossed a rejuvenated Elvis into one story (Time in a Little Blue Bottle) to give it a little peanut butter crunch! Savor them all but start now. More are coming, and you don't want to get too far behind!

Contact information:

Email: dani@danihaviland.com

Twitter: @dani_haviland

I love to hear from readers!

Sign up for my newsletter to get the latest information on new releases, free stuff, and contests at: http://bit.ly/2DHnews

Awesome readers make up a street team!

I have a Facebook Page for folks who are interested in early excerpts and insights into my latest books and box sets. I'd appreciate a like on the page. Drop in and see if I've remembered to add photos and excerpts of my works in process. http://bit.ly/2DaniStTeam

www.ingramcontent.com/pod-product-compliance
Lightning Source LLC
Chambersburg PA
CBHW082010170626
46817CB00009B/3053

9781946752642